ANNIVERSARY EDITION

THOROUGHBRED

THE BESTSELLING SERIES!

Ashleigh's Hope

CREATED BY
JOANNA CAMPBELL

Ashleigh discovers her dream.

Harper
Paperbacks

U.S. $3.99
CAN.$4.99

ISBN 0-06-106395-9

9 780061 063954

50399

Ashleigh loved her riding lessons—
except for one thing . . .

Ashleigh carefully wiped down the saddle with liquid saddle soap and a soft cloth. While she was buffing the saddle to a high gloss, she heard voices coming down the aisle.

"Are they gone?" Diana asked.

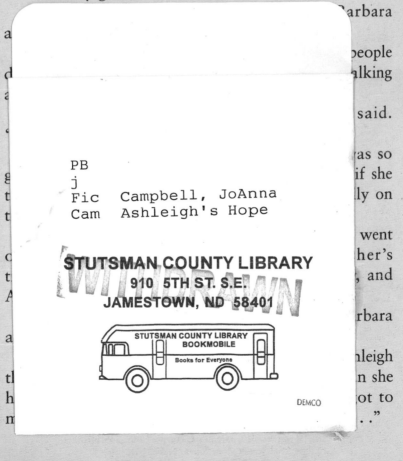

Don't miss these exciting books from HarperPaperbacks!

Collect all the books in the THOROUGHBRED series:

THOROUGHBRED

ASHLEIGH'S HOPE

WRITTEN BY
KAREN BENTLEY

CREATED BY
JOANNA CAMPBELL

HarperPaperbacks

A Division of HarperCollins*Publishers*

HarperPaperbacks *A Division of* HarperCollins*Publishers*
10 East 53rd Street, New York, N.Y. 10022

Copyright © 1996 by Daniel Weiss Associates, Inc.,
and Joanna Campbell
Cover art copyright © 1996 Daniel Weiss Associates, Inc.

First printing: April 1996

Printed in the United States of America

HarperPaperbacks and colophon are trademarks of HarperCollins*Publishers*

❖ 10 9 8 7 6 5 4 3 2 1

For John

ASHLEIGH'S HOPE

1

"GO, GALLANTRY," TEN-YEAR-OLD ASHLEIGH GRIFFEN shouted, jumping to her feet. "Run for it!" The bay Thoroughbred mare thundered down the stretch at Churchill Downs, her black mane whipping in the crisp late October air. Eight other Thoroughbred mares roared after her in the six-furlong race. The distant drumming of their hooves grew deafening as they pounded around the turn, heading for the finish.

Gallantry was within a furlong of winning her first race. Afterward she would return with the Griffens to Edgardale, their breeding farm near Lexington. Ashleigh's parents had claimed the horse for ten thousand dollars before the race. From the moment the starting bell clanged, she had belonged to the Griffens.

"And it's Gallantry, staging a big stretch run," the announcer called.

Ashleigh stared across the infield at the track. Now if Gallantry could just hold off her challengers!

"Run, Gallantry, run!" shouted Rory, Ashleigh's five-year-old brother, as he stared intently at the field. Ashleigh doubted that Rory really knew what was at stake, but he imitated almost everything she did.

Flying Irish, a big black mare, suddenly drove by the tiring pacesetters. She matched strides down the stretch with Gallantry.

Ashleigh leaned forward, willing Gallantry to win. She had never ridden a Thoroughbred, only ponies and mixed breeds, but she could almost feel what it would be like to be on one of those magnificent racehorses. She'd be balanced over the horse's withers in the featherlight racing saddle, her hands buried in the mane as she asked for a final burst of speed. Riding so close to the horse, she'd be as one with it as they plunged to victory.

"Flying Irish is going to catch her!" groaned Ashleigh's thirteen-year-old sister, Caroline. In her tweed coat and stylish black derby, she fit in well with the sophisticated race-goers at Churchill Downs.

"No, she won't catch her!" Ashleigh said. Flying Irish had found her best stride too late—Gallantry was holding off Irish's late run! Ashleigh couldn't believe the length of Gallantry's strides as she changed leads. Ashleigh had seen dozens of races, but nothing was so exciting to her as the moment when a Thoroughbred switched into high gear in the stretch and powered for the finish.

The mare swept under the wire. "And Gallantry runs an unexpectedly strong race as a forty-three-to-one outsider," the announcer shouted. "She wins it by two lengths."

"Incredible!" Beaming, Ashleigh turned to her mother and father.

"I can't think of a better way to start the fall meet at Churchill Downs," Elaine Griffen said, bending to fold up their picnic blanket. "We certainly got our money's worth with Gallantry."

"She ran a strong race," Derek Griffen said proudly. Ashleigh had gotten her dark hair and hazel eyes from her father. Rory and Caroline had their mother's fair coloring.

Ashleigh's parents were as crazy about horses as she was. Two years before, the Griffens had all saved and scrimped to buy Edgardale, their small breeding farm. Mrs. Griffen still had her office job in Lexington, but Ashleigh knew her mom hoped to quit it soon and devote all her time to the ten broodmares and seven weanlings at Edgardale.

"So why was the announcer surprised that Gallantry won?" Ashleigh asked her parents.

"She lost her last four races pretty badly," Mr. Griffen said. "But I watched three of them, and I still thought she had talent. She really lost most of those races by accident—she broke badly from the gate, she drew a poor post position, or the jockey didn't ride well."

"Let's go get her," Ashleigh said eagerly.

"We will!" Mrs. Griffen laughed. "Believe me, we're not going to leave her unattended for long. She's our horse now, no matter what happens. But her former owners get to stand with her in the winner's circle and collect the purse money."

"How come?" Ashleigh was disappointed.

Her mother shrugged. "That's just how claiming a horse works."

"Let's go watch." Ashleigh hurried across the infield ahead of her family. The elegant twin spires of the renowned racetrack of Churchill Downs soared above the wire, where Gallantry had just run to victory.

The stream of jockeys and their mounts from the race passed in front of Ashleigh, headed for the tunnel to the backside. Dressed in the brightly colored silks of the horses' stables, the jockeys were talking with one another and with the trainers and grooms who had come out to the track to meet them. To Ashleigh, even being at Churchill Downs was a thrill. This was where the finest Thoroughbreds in the world raced, ridden by the best jockeys.

I wish that was me on one of those horses, Ashleigh thought. *But I have a long way to go before I can ride racehorses here.*

In the winner's circle beside the track, Gallantry's former owners were posing with the mare for the cameras. The bay mare was breathing easily, as if she'd just gone for a gallop instead of pounded through a three-quarter-mile race. After two years of living on a Thoroughbred breeding farm, Ashleigh immediately noted the perfect angle of the Thoroughbred's sleek shoulders and her slender but powerful legs.

Gallantry pawed the ground lightly and flung up her head. The horse's dark eyes focused on Ashleigh.

Ashleigh stared back. She remembered the weird feeling

she'd had during the race—that she was riding the horse, not just watching her. *I feel like I'm standing in the winner's circle now,* Ashleigh thought.

Rory rushed up to her, clutching a lead rope. "This is for Gallantry after they take her picture," he said. "I'm going to lead her to the trailer."

Ashleigh looked at her little brother, startled. The spell was broken. Gallantry wasn't her racehorse. "No, I am," she said quickly. "I'm older."

"*I'm* going to lead her," Mrs. Griffen said firmly. "Let's go, kids. We'll pick up the mare in the receiving barn."

Ashleigh walked to the track backside after her parents and Caroline. It was late morning, and the backside was busy. Allowance races and a stakes race, in which the horses ran against better competition and for more money, were still to come on the card that afternoon. Beautiful horses of every color, with the clean lines and finely sculpted heads characteristic of Thoroughbreds, paced behind their grooms, going to and from the barns. Some of the horses moved in circles on hot-walkers, powerful machines with spokes like a horizontal Ferris wheel. The horses were attached to the spokes by lead lines.

As Ashleigh watched, a coal-black stallion on one of the hot-walkers suddenly dug in his heels, shook his head with a squeal of annoyance, and tried to drag the hot-walker the other way. Two grooms rushed to calm him.

"That's Triple Derby," Mrs. Griffen said. "He must be here for the Breeders' Cup races next Saturday. He won the Classic last year."

"What a beautiful horse," Caroline said admiringly.

"Yeah," Rory agreed. "He shines like a black star."

"He's Zip Away's half-brother, isn't he?" Ashleigh asked. Zip Away was one of Edgardale's mares.

"Yes—we were very lucky to get Zip Away when we did," Mr. Griffen answered. "We paid only twenty-five hundred dollars for her at the Ocala Breeders' auction a year and a half ago. After Triple Derby won a Breeders' Cup race, her value went up quite a bit."

It would be so great to have a horse like Triple Derby, Ashleigh thought wistfully. She knew he cost a fortune, though. Zip Away might be related to him, but owning her wasn't nearly the same as owning a horse about to run in the Breeders' Cup. Zip Away was just a broodmare now.

Ashleigh walked along with her family past the barns, but she kept her eyes on the gorgeous stallion. "Dad, can we buy me a horse next?" she asked.

"Ashleigh, we've been over this again and again." Mr. Griffen sighed. "Not right now—the farm is still on a shoestring budget. We're buying Gallantry as an investment, not a luxury. Besides, you've got Moe."

"Moe isn't exactly a racehorse," Ashleigh pointed out. "He's eleven hands high."

Mr. Griffen laughed. "He's pretty fast for a Shetland, isn't he?" He looked at her curiously. "Why do you need a racehorse?"

Ashleigh hesitated. "I like them," she said. "They're so fast and beautiful."

"We'll see what our yearlings go for at the Keeneland

January auction," Mr. Griffen said. "Until then, there's no way we can buy *or* keep a pleasure horse."

Ashleigh nodded and looked away. She doubted that her parents would have more money after the auction. They might make a decent amount, but extra money always went for something like vet bills. *Maybe they'll make loads and loads of money at the auction this year. I guess that's all I can hope for,* she thought.

In the receiving barn a short, wiry man with black hair held Gallantry. "Heard this is your horse," he called to the Griffens. "I'm Joe Gibbons—I train at Fairhill Acres."

"Thanks for your efforts with the mare," Mr. Griffen said. "Her performance today was impressive."

"I thought so, too. I think she was just coming into her own as a racehorse, but she should make a fine broodmare as well. Good luck," the trainer said. He handed Gallantry's lead line to Mrs. Griffen.

The mare half reared, almost yanking the line through Mrs. Griffen's hands. "Steady, girl," Mrs. Griffen soothed. She jerked on the line and quickly got the mare moving toward the Griffens' trailer.

Ashleigh ran to catch up with her mother. Gallantry danced on her toes, snorting softly. Her sleek bay coat flashed in the muted fall sunlight. "Can I lead her?" Ashleigh asked.

"Not right now," Mrs. Griffen said. "You handle horses better than almost anyone I know, Ashleigh, but you're only ten. Gallantry doesn't know you yet, and she's still excited from the race. You can help with her once we get her home and settled."

Ashleigh watched the mare's powerful shoulder muscles bunch and release as she walked to the trailer. Gallantry was a big horse, probably sixteen hands, but her steps were light and quick.

I've never been this close to a horse that just won a race, Ashleigh thought. Gallantry arched her neck, then reached over to bump Ashleigh.

"Watch out!" Caroline warned.

"She's okay." Ashleigh laid a soothing hand on Gallantry's glossy shoulder. "You know that you won today, don't you? You just feel good."

Mr. Griffen unlatched the door to the trailer. The big mare hesitated, then bounded inside. Mr. Griffen quickly shut the door behind her.

"It's almost a shame to retire her," he said. "After the performance she put in today, she could go into a bigger claiming race or maybe even do well in an allowance race. But we don't have the facilities or money to train her for racing."

"With her bloodlines, she'll make a wonderful broodmare," Mrs. Griffen reminded him.

The beautiful mare shifted uneasily in the trailer stall. Ashleigh climbed up on the trailer hitch and opened the front window to make sure she had enough water and hay. Gallantry snorted and stretched her neck to sniff Ashleigh. "It's okay," Ashleigh said softly. "Wait till you see your new home. You won't believe how wonderful it is. And you'll have lots of other horses for company."

Gallantry stamped her foot. The trailer swayed up and down.

"Easy, girl," Ashleigh said. Ashleigh's family had already gotten into the truck, and she was alone with the mare. Gallantry pushed backward against the trailer door, trying to get out. *I'll bet you want to run some more. I wish you could. I'd love to ride you in a race,* Ashleigh thought.

She reached to rub the mare's small star. "Someday I'll ride a horse like you—a Thoroughbred," she said. "Then I'll race my horse at Churchill Downs. I know I will."

The mare was quiet now. She had her ears flicked back, listening.

"Ashleigh!" Mr. Griffen yelled from the truck cab. "Let's go!"

"Okay!" Ashleigh called back, giving the mare's soft muzzle a last pat. "See you soon, girl." Ashleigh ran to get in the truck with her family.

2

ON THE DRIVE HOME FROM THE TRACK, ASHLEIGH looked out the window at the brilliant green pastures of Kentucky horse country. The white-fenced paddocks were filled with horses, mostly Thoroughbreds, cropping grass in the afternoon sunshine.

I can't wait to get home and ride, she thought. She always wanted to saddle up her own pony after a day at the races. Moe might be small, but her dad was right—Moe *was* fast for a Shetland. He was a lot of fun to ride.

The truck bumped onto a gravel road. Now the well-kept paddocks on both sides were Edgardale's, and the seven bright-eyed Thoroughbred weanlings romping in the side paddock were the Griffens'. So were the ten mares grazing in the big front paddock, swishing their tails as they munched the lush grass. Ashleigh leaned forward eagerly, ready to jump out of the truck the second it stopped.

Sunstorm, a big gray weanling out of Zip Away, jerked up his head and snorted in surprise as the Griffens' truck and trailer rattled by. Suddenly he began to race alongside the paddock fence.

"Sunstorm thinks he's going to beat us!" Ashleigh said. The gray horse's black-and-white mane and tail streamed in the breeze as he lengthened his stride to keep up with the truck.

"I never saw a horse race a truck before," Mrs. Griffen remarked.

"Do you think we can put that in the program when he goes to auction?" Mr. Griffen chuckled.

Ashleigh frowned. Auctions weren't her favorite subject. She had learned to accept that the foals at Edgardale belonged to the Griffens only until they were yearlings. Then they were sold at auction, because Edgardale didn't have the training facilities to bring them along as racehorses. Ashleigh decided that no matter how long she lived on a breeding farm, she'd never like selling the horses.

Mr. Griffen slowed the truck as he neared the end of Sunstorm's paddock. The colt charged in front.

Ashleigh watched nervously. "I hope he doesn't go right through the fence!"

"He won't," Mr. Griffen said. "He's got too much sense for that."

Sunstorm skidded to a stop just in front of the white boards. Kicking up his heels smartly, the colt trotted off to rejoin the other weanlings.

"He thinks he won," Caroline said as they climbed out of the truck.

Ashleigh grinned. "Sunstorm's my favorite weanling," she said. "He's feisty."

"How would you like to help me gentle him?" Mrs. Griffen suggested.

"Sure!" Ashleigh said excitedly. Ashleigh's parents worked with the young horses as much as possible, because the more they were handled at this age, the easier they'd be to manage when they were thousand-pound racehorses. Ashleigh had played with the weanlings in the paddock, but she'd never been given real responsibility for gentling a weanling before. She'd been begging for years to help out, but her parents had always said she was too young.

"I want to try to get Sunstorm and Southern Sky ready for the Keeneland mixed sale in January," Mrs. Griffen said. "If they bring a good price there, we might be able to buy another mare in time for next year's breeding season."

Ashleigh sighed. She didn't want her favorite weanling to be sold. But if it had to happen, at least she could be with him as much as possible before then.

"Come on, girl," Mrs. Griffen said to Gallantry, carefully easing the mare backward out of the trailer. Gallantry jumped off the edge of the ramp and stood stock still, snorting. Mrs. Griffen let her take a look at the huge brown barn that housed all the mares and younger horses, the feed-storage sheds, and the acres and acres of tempting grass.

Gallantry suddenly hauled on the lead rope, half dragging Mrs. Griffen toward the mares' paddock.

Caroline jumped out of the way. "That horse is scary. If

nobody needs me, I think I'll go up to the house and call one of my friends," she said.

Ashleigh stared at her sister in surprise. *What's Caroline scared of?* she wondered. "Gallantry's upset because this is a new place," she said. "She's just acting like a normal horse."

"That's what I mean—she's scary," Caroline said.

Mrs. Griffen pulled firmly on Gallantry's lead line. The big mare reluctantly halted. "Go ahead, Caroline," she said. "We're pretty much done here." Caroline walked up to the Griffens' old stone farmhouse.

"Can Gallantry go out with the other mares?" Ashleigh asked. The placid mares in foal had stopped grazing and were all watching the newcomer. Ashleigh couldn't imagine putting a fireball like Gallantry in with them.

"I'll put her out by herself until she calms down," Mrs. Griffen said, opening the gate to the five-acre paddock next to the mares' paddock. The bay horse rushed through and galloped to the far fence. "Ashleigh, would you watch her for a few minutes and see how she does? I've got to go to my office in town."

"But it's Saturday," Ashleigh said.

"Well, I've got a lot of work to do." Mrs. Griffen sighed. "I'm not exactly happy about it. I won't be back until after dinner, I'm afraid."

"We'll help you with the chores, Dad," Rory said.

"Sure," Ashleigh agreed. "I'm going for a ride with Mona after Gallantry settles down, but we won't be long. I just want to give Moe some exercise and tell Mona about the races." Mona was Ashleigh's best friend. She rode her Shetland pony, Toby, with Ashleigh almost every day.

"Okay, I'll start the chores at about four. I'm counting on you kids to help." Mr. Griffen smiled.

Ashleigh walked over to Gallantry's paddock and climbed onto the bottom board of the fence to watch her. The bay mare frantically galloped up and down the paddock, skidding to a stop every time she reached a fence. Her unhappy whinnies pierced the air.

"Whoa, baby," Ashleigh called. She didn't want Gallantry to work herself up any more. She might go through the fence or trip, wrenching a leg. But Gallantry didn't seem to have any intention of settling down. The high-strung racehorse looked out of place next to the calm, peacefully munching mothers-to-be in the adjoining paddock.

"I know, this must seem kind of quiet after the track," Ashleigh murmured. "But the other horses like it here, Gallantry. You will, too. At least I think you will if you try."

Jolita, a tall black mare, walked over to the fence separating the paddocks. The two horses touched noses. At last, huffing out a little snort, Gallantry bent her head and took a quick bite of grass.

Good, Ashleigh thought. *I think she'll be okay now.* Ashleigh jumped off the fence and walked over to the weanling paddock to get Moe. She didn't see him, but the little pony was somewhere in there.

As Ashleigh approached, the young horses stopped grazing and stood like statues, watching her. She opened the gate and walked over to Sunstorm. The gray colt

14

lowered his head and nuzzled her hands, then propped his head affectionately on her shoulder. Sunstorm was already taller than she was.

Ashleigh rubbed his muzzle. "You're just a teddy bear, aren't you?" she asked. "I think it'll be easy to gentle you."

The other weanlings crowded around, nibbling at Ashleigh's shirt and nudging her. Ashleigh tried to pat as many soft noses and sleek dapple, chestnut, and black necks as possible. She knew all the young horses so well. She'd helped to take care of them since they were born the previous spring, and she'd talked and played with them for hours. She'd even seen Jill-in-the-Box, an exquisite black filly, being born and take her first shaky, triumphant steps.

Ashleigh loved her life around horses. Sometimes she thought it was almost too good to be true that she lived on a Thoroughbred breeding farm. Every morning she woke up at Edgardale, with seventeen horses right outside her bedroom window. Except for when she was at school, she was surrounded by horses.

Moe peered around Sunstorm's flank. "There you are, pony," Ashleigh said with relief.

Sunstorm looked around at Moe and pinned back his ears. He picked up a hind leg, threatening to kick. Moe backed away hastily.

Ashleigh frowned. The chocolate-colored Shetland was so small, even the weanlings pushed him around. But Moe pined if he was put out by himself.

Ashleigh looked at Sunstorm for a second. The

muscular colt, with his finely sculpted head and small, well-shaped ears, looked a lot like his uncle Triple Derby. That was a good sign—he might have his uncle's speed, too. "I wish I could see you run," she said. "But I'll have to wait until you're on the track, since you're going to auction in January."

Ashleigh frowned. A good ride on Moe would put the subject of auctions out of her mind for a while. "Be nice to Moe, Sunstorm," she ordered. "You're a lot bigger than he is." Ashleigh pushed through the weanlings and stretched out her hand with a carrot in it to Moe. The pony took a step back. But his intelligent dark eyes were fixed on the carrot.

"Come on, little guy," Ashleigh coaxed, walking toward him.

Moe stood motionless. Ashleigh knew the pony was deciding whether he wanted the carrot enough to let her catch him. Moe liked to spend his afternoons grazing and napping.

Ashleigh waited patiently, holding out the carrot. Finally Moe made up his mind. With a toss of his small head, the pony stepped toward her.

"Got you," Ashleigh said, slipping on the halter and smoothing Moe's thick forelock out of his eyes. She led her pony to the gate and expertly shut it behind them before any of the weanlings could follow. The weanlings gathered around the gate, watching Ashleigh. "I'll come get you in a little while and feed you," she promised.

In the barn the twenty-four big, roomy box stalls were empty. At this time of day all the horses were out in the

16

paddocks. At night the mares occupied ten stalls and the weanlings seven. Ashleigh's parents hoped someday to buy enough quality mares to fill this barn and then build another barn to house the younger horses.

That hadn't happened yet. But that night Gallantry would fill another stall, Ashleigh reminded herself.

Ashleigh crosstied Moe in the concrete aisle, quickly brushed the pony's heavy coat, and tacked him up. She and Mona had agreed to meet at three at the top of the lane behind Edgardale. It was almost three now.

"We've got to hurry," Ashleigh told Moe as she quickly mounted. Moe broke into a brisk trot the moment they left the stable yard. Once he was saddled up and away from the paddock, Moe was a frisky little guy.

I'll bet this isn't much like riding a Thoroughbred, Ashleigh thought, trying to relax her back enough to take the impact of Moe's short strides. Her feet almost touched the ground. "I *am* getting too big for you," she said sadly. "I guess someday I'll have to give you to a little kid like Rory." Ashleigh leaned over and buried her face in his thick, soft mane. "But I love you," she murmured. Moe had been her pony since she was five. Ashleigh couldn't imagine selling him, whether she got too big to ride him or not. She urged him into a canter.

"Ashleigh!" Mona called. She was riding Toby, her black Shetland. Dark-haired and athletically built, Mona could have been Ashleigh's sister. The resemblance was more than skin deep—Mona was as wild about horses as Ashleigh was. Both girls had been riding for most of their lives.

"Guess what!" Ashleigh said as she pulled Moe up beside them. "My parents bought Gallantry—and then she won her race!" Ashleigh had already told Mona about the Griffens' plan to add the mare to their stock.

"Cool!" Mona said. "How's she doing?"

"She looks great. But she hasn't really settled in yet." Ashleigh frowned. "Maybe she will soon. You could come see her tomorrow. What do you want to do now?"

"Ride," Mona said with a laugh.

"I *know* that," Ashleigh said. "Let's go through the woods."

The girls guided Moe and Toby under the colorful trees. At the same instant both ponies broke into a trot.

Ashleigh sat deep in the saddle and sniffed the air, faintly scented with wood smoke. The sky was a deep turquoise and dotted with small white clouds. Moe plowed through piles of brilliant red and yellow leaves that had blown up against the trees.

Riding in the fall is so perfect, Ashleigh thought.

Mona trotted Toby up beside them. "Did you start your science paper yet?" she asked.

"No. But it's not due until next week." Ashleigh didn't want to think about the science paper. It was going to be a major effort. Mr. Gates, Ashleigh's fifth-grade teacher, would expect original research. For a second Ashleigh wondered if she could just look up somebody such as Madame Curie in the encyclopedia and paraphrase a couple of sentences about her. But she knew she'd have to do better than that.

Moe splashed through a clear, cold stream laced with

fallen leaves. In a still pool Ashleigh caught a glimpse of her reflection. She was sitting up straight in the saddle, in her black boots and hard hat.

I look good, Ashleigh thought. *I wonder how good a rider I really am.* She knew she rode Moe well, but riding a Shetland pony wasn't like riding a dressage horse, or a show-jumping horse, or a racehorse.

Moe craned his neck around and looked at her affectionately. Ashleigh leaned forward and hugged him. "You're my very own wonderful pony," she assured him. "I don't ever want to give you up."

"You either," Mona said to Toby.

Ashleigh sat back in the saddle and tightened the reins. "Let's canter!" she said, urging Moe up the bank of the creek. The pony leaped into the faster pace when she squeezed her legs. Ashleigh heard the staccato beat of Toby's small hooves right behind them. They burst out of the woods back onto the grassy lane.

Suddenly Toby drew even with them, then shot into the lead.

The sharp October wind whipped back Ashleigh's hair. "We won't let you get away with that!" she called to Mona.

A turn was coming up. Mona let Toby take it a little wide. Ashleigh saw her chance. The opening on the inside was narrow, but she thought she could squeak Moe through it—if he would go.

She needn't have worried. The game little pony plunged through the opening and drew ahead of Toby. Now if they could just stay ahead!

Moe seemed to understand. He was loving the race. With a snort he changed leads and galloped even faster. Ashleigh pulled him up only when they reached the edge of the next stand of woods. By that time they were far in the lead.

"Way to go, boy!" she praised him.

"No fair!" Mona called as she rode up on Toby. "I had to let you go through on that turn—I was afraid I'd run into you."

"It's fair as long as I don't bump you. Then it would be interference," Ashleigh said. "At least that's what they'd call it at the track."

Mona looked angry.

"I'm sorry," Ashleigh said. "I guess I got a little carried away."

"You acted like we were running in a real race. Which one was it?" Mona asked, laughing.

Ashleigh smiled back. She was glad Mona wasn't angry with her anymore. "The Breeders' Cup Classic," she answered. "After the Kentucky Derby, that's the biggest race of the year."

3

"I'VE GOT A SURPRISE FOR YOU GIRLS," MR. GRIFFEN SAID
at dinner that night. "I think you're going to like it.
Especially you, Ashleigh."

Ashleigh looked up from her bowl of tomato soup. Her
dad looked excited, as though this surprise was a big one.
"You got me a horse," she said.

Mr. Griffen laughed. "Ashleigh, you have a one-track
mind. No, I didn't get you a horse. But your mom and I
arranged for you and Caroline to take riding lessons over
at Chesterton Riding Academy."

Ashleigh felt a growing bubble of excitement. Riding
lessons! This was fantastic news.

"Wow!" Caroline raised her eyebrows. "Chesterton is a
high-class place!"

"Yeah, it is," Ashleigh agreed. "A bunch of the rich kids
in my class take lessons there. They board their horses
there, too."

"You'll have to ride school horses for now," Mr. Griffen said. "We do expect to get both of you horses someday. Our crop of weanlings is outstanding this year, and we may have some extra money after the January auction."

"Wow!" Ashleigh gasped.

"But the first step toward owning a horse is learning to ride well," Mr. Griffen said.

"I can't wait to take lessons!" Ashleigh said. She was already imagining the school horse she would ride. It might be a Thoroughbred, reconditioned from the track, or one of the big European warmbloods. Maybe she would get a chestnut, her favorite color of horse. When she got her very own horse, it would definitely be a chestnut, she decided.

"I hope I do okay at the lessons," Caroline said. She sounded worried.

Ashleigh jerked out of her daydreams. "You'll love them," she said with conviction. "It'll be so much fun!"

"The kids who ride at Chesterton are supposed to be really good," Caroline said. "I can't even stop Moe from running away with me."

"Moe's pretty stubborn." Ashleigh grinned. She remembered the last time the short-legged little pony had seized the bit in his teeth and taken off with Caroline. Caroline had been screeching at him to stop, but Moe had galloped a good half mile before she managed to pull him up.

"How often can we take lessons?" Ashleigh asked her dad.

"We've signed you up for two hours twice a week—

after school on Tuesdays and on Saturday afternoons. Part of the deal, though, is that you and Caroline will be responsible for your school horses' care on the days you ride. You'll groom them, clean their tack, and muck out their stalls."

"No problem," Ashleigh said happily. She hadn't thought her parents would be able to afford lessons more than once a week. With so many lessons, she'd be sure to make fast progress.

Caroline, she noticed, was wincing at the mention of cleaning out stalls. Caro usually managed to get out of stall-cleaning duty at home by offering to do household chores.

Rory finished his soup and looked at their father. "I want to take riding lessons, too," he said.

"When you're older," Mr. Griffen said.

"Please?" Rory begged. "I'm never older."

"Don't be silly, Rory," Caroline said. "Of course you're older—every year."

"We don't have enough money for all three of you to take lessons now," Mr. Griffen said. "You can have lessons when you're ten, Rory, like Ashleigh. Until then you have to wait."

Rory dropped his head into his hands and knocked over the salt shaker with his elbow. Salt poured across the table.

"That was dumb," Caroline said.

Rory put the salt shaker back upright and looked away.

"I'll clean it up. Let him alone, Caro," Ashleigh said quickly. She knew what was wrong with Rory—he felt left

23

out. It was tough to be the youngest. "I know, Rory. I'll teach you to ride Moe," she offered.

"Do you mean it?" Rory asked, his face alight.

"Of course. It'll be fun." Ashleigh looked fondly at her little brother. *Maybe someday he'll love Moe as much as I do*, she thought. *Riding lessons are a great present to give anyone.* Ashleigh smiled at her father.

"Thanks for the lessons, Dad," she said.

"You're welcome, sweetie." Mr. Griffen smiled back. "I think you'll get a lot out of them—your school horse is part Thoroughbred, and he's had years of dressage training."

"That is so cool!" Ashleigh couldn't believe her luck.

She carried her dishes to the sink and stacked them. It was her turn to clean up the kitchen that night, but first she wanted to go out to the barn. She hadn't told Sunstorm yet that they would be working together. Besides, she wanted to tell all the horses the good news about the riding lessons and say good night to them.

The night sky over the farm was clear and sprinkled with stars. Ashleigh stepped gratefully into the warm barn, rubbing her chilly bare arms. It smelled of hay, sweet feed, and clean, contented horses.

The barn was quiet except for the occasional stamp of a restless horse. At this time of night most of the mares and weanlings would be dozing in their stalls, tired out from a day of sunshine and play. The younger horses were at the far end of the barn. Ashleigh tiptoed down the aisle, looking in at the mares by the dim glow of the night-lights.

Wanderer put her head over the stall door and looked at Ashleigh inquiringly. "Hi, pretty girl," Ashleigh whispered.

24

Ashleigh knew that of all the mares, her parents had the highest hopes for Wanderer. They had bought her the previous winter, then bred her to an outstanding stallion that had already sired several stakes winners.

But nobody really knew which mares would have champion offspring. Ashleigh knew that was part of the excitement of a breeding farm—when it didn't drive her parents crazy with worry that they'd guessed wrong in breeding the mares.

Gallantry's stall was just after the broodmares'. The bay mare was pacing, turning sharply every time she was confronted by a wall. When she saw Ashleigh, she walked over to the half-door and looked out, tossing her head.

"You haven't calmed down much, have you?" Ashleigh frowned. "Did you eat?" She checked the mare's feed bucket. Gallantry had eaten about half of her grain.

"At least you ate some," Ashleigh said, reaching to stroke the mare. Nervous horses often wouldn't eat anything at all.

Gallantry backed away and resumed her pacing. Ashleigh had thought the mare would have settled down by now. But it was only Gallantry's first day on the farm. She probably just needed a little more time.

Ashleigh looked in on Sunstorm. The sleek gray colt lay sprawled on the straw. He lifted his head and sleepily flicked an ear at her.

"Don't wake up," Ashleigh whispered. "I just wanted to look at you."

But Sunstorm got up, shook out his mane, stretched, and walked over to the stall door.

Ashleigh took his soft black muzzle in her hands. "Guess what," she said. "I'll be helping to gentle you. I've got a lot of ideas about what we should do. We'll work every day, except when I have riding lessons."

Ashleigh leaned against the stall door and tried to imagine what the riding lessons would be like. She really had no idea. The riding school was said to have beautifully trained equitation horses, jumpers, and dressage horses. For a moment Ashleigh pictured herself on a Lippizaner, performing a passage.

Sunstorm nipped her hand, as if to bring her back to reality. "You're right—I probably won't be doing a passage right away," Ashleigh said with a laugh. "It's easier to imagine working with you. That will be so much fun. Except it's not so good why I'm doing it. It's to get you ready for the auction in January."

Sunstorm rested his chin on Ashleigh's shoulder and sighed. His breath was sweet, smelling of hay.

"I know. I feel sad about it, too," Ashleigh said. "Someone else will put you into training and ride you. Meanwhile I'll be riding school horses at Chesterton. I hope I do okay."

Ashleigh narrowed her hazel eyes thoughtfully. She had always considered herself a good rider. She hardly ever fell off, and she'd ridden Moe for years. Before that, she'd ridden every chance she got—on ponies at carnivals, on a scruffy big pony in the yard next to the Griffens' old house in town, and on merry-go-round horses when she was very small and couldn't find a real horse. But her riding had never been evaluated by a professional.

"I wonder what the instructor will think," she said.

The gray colt backed away from the stall door. He huffed out a little sigh and relaxed, standing on three legs.

"I know, it's time for bed," Ashleigh agreed. "Get a lot of sleep, boy. We've got work to do. We'll do fine."

I bet I'll do well at Chesterton next week, too, she thought happily as she walked out of the shadowy barn.

"I can't believe Diana," Mona said on Monday at school. She pointed across the cafeteria. "Look at that show-off."

Ashleigh glanced over at the doorway. Diana Carruthers had just stolen Rick Metz's baseball cap and put it backward on her head. Rick tried to grab his cap, but Diana threw it to Barbara Richards.

Diana and her friends were the most popular group in the fifth grade. They were the stars of the soccer team and practically ran the school. They teased the boys all the time, pretending they had boyfriends.

Ashleigh shrugged. "Just because Diana thinks she's the coolest kid at school doesn't mean I do."

"Yeah, but have you ever seen her horse?" Mona asked. "It's awesome."

"I will tomorrow, when my riding lessons start. Diana boards her horse at Chesterton, and she's in my class." Ashleigh unwrapped her sandwich and took a bite. "I know all about Diana's horse already. Her dad paid ten thousand dollars for it, and an Olympic gold medalist trained it to jump. The whole school knows everything about that horse because Diana won't stop bragging about it."

"I don't know if I'd really want to take lessons at Chesterton," Mona said. "It's supposed to be an incredible riding school, but all the kids who take lessons there are so stuck up. My parents are talking about buying me my own horse. Then I could just learn to ride it myself or take private lessons."

"My parents can't afford that," Ashleigh said.

"Sorry—I didn't mean to sound like I was bragging," Mona said quickly.

"That's okay. I think Edgardale is going to do great someday. My parents are breeding the mares really carefully, and some of the weanlings look fantastic. But I have to wait to get my own horse."

"Oh, no—here comes Diana," Mona hissed.

Ashleigh looked up in surprise. Diana and her group were heading toward their table, laughing and talking loudly. Ashleigh realized she hadn't even spoken to Diana in about a year, since fourth-grade soccer tryouts. Ashleigh had beaten Diana out for starting center but then quit because she wanted to spend more time at home with the horses. Diana was the center on the soccer team now.

Diana slid onto the bench next to her. "Hi," she said. She sounded friendly.

"Hi." Ashleigh couldn't help noticing Diana's clothes. Diana wore an expensive oversized sweater with matching leggings. The unusual dark brown and gold of her outfit matched her big brown eyes and blond hair. Ashleigh guessed Diana was pretty. Most of the kids at school seemed to think so.

"I heard from our instructor that you and your sister are starting riding lessons at Chesterton tomorrow," Diana said. "I have just one question."

"What?" Ashleigh asked. Diana didn't look so friendly now.

"How did you get in? The school is supposed to be exclusive. I mean, for people who, well . . ." Diana looked at her friends and grinned. "Who have their own horses to ride."

Barbara giggled.

Mona rolled her eyes. "What's so funny?" she asked.

"Nothing," Barbara said. "Are you bringing your own horse for the lessons, Ashleigh?"

"I hadn't planned to." Ashleigh knew the girls were trying to get to her, but the conversation wasn't really bothering her. She couldn't care less what Diana and her snobby friends thought.

"My horse, Silverado, is a Dutch warmblood," Diana said. "My father bought him in Europe. Silverado is a champion jumper."

"I heard," Ashleigh said. *So what?* she thought. *Every single horse at Edgardale is worth more than hers. Probably more talented, too.*

"I've got a Hanoverian," said Cheryl Marshall, another of Diana's friends.

"Big horse," Ashleigh commented. In her opinion someone as short as Cheryl didn't belong on a Hanoverian, but it wasn't worth it to Ashleigh to point this out. "Have you had lunch?" she asked. "The lunch line is about to close." She hoped they would get the hint.

"Ashleigh, I don't want to be mean, but I really should say this." Diana leaned closer. "I think you and your sister are going to be a little outclassed at our lessons. You've never had lessons at all, have you?"

"I've ridden my pony for years," Ashleigh said.

Diana shook her head. "At our last lesson our instructor said that your parents think you're some kind of star rider. But riding a pony isn't anything like riding a real horse. Plus, at Chesterton you'll be riding stable nags."

"I heard about the horse I'll be riding," Ashleigh said. "Ranger's a great horse."

Diana snorted. "He's a smart stable nag, that's about all I can say for him."

"I'm sure he'll be fine," Ashleigh said, picking up her sandwich again.

"Well, I guess I can't talk you out of it." Diana shrugged. "So we'll just see how it goes."

"Yeah." Ashleigh wondered why Diana was trying to psych her out. *Maybe she's afraid of the competition,* she thought. *But that's hard to believe. I'm not going to be riding a horse anywhere near as good as hers.*

"Diana—sit over here!" Kimberly Aston called. She and several other kids on the girls' soccer team waved.

Diana swung her legs over the bench. "See you at the lesson—if you decide to come after all," she said.

Ashleigh and Mona watched Diana rejoin her friends. Then they looked at each other and burst out laughing. "Can you believe them?" Mona asked. "They're awful."

"I'm not sure how much fun it's going to be to take riding lessons with them," Ashleigh said.

4

ASHLEIGH SAID GOOD-BYE TO HER MOTHER IN FRONT OF THE elaborate wrought-iron stable gate at Chesterton Riding Academy. "This place is incredible!" she said to Caroline.

On each side of the drive was a huge outdoor ring. In one of the rings two riders, sitting straight on flat saddles, paced their horses through the slow, elegant piaffe of dressage.

In the other ring a hunt class was forming. A line of tall, athletic-looking horses wearing hunt saddles walked across the drive with their riders. A few of the riders nodded a greeting to Caroline and Ashleigh, but most of them already looked focused on the lesson ahead.

In the hunt-class ring a girl about Ashleigh's age was effortlessly taking her horse over a four-foot wall. *Wow,* Ashleigh thought as she opened the gate. "Look at the size of those jumps!" she said to Caroline.

Caroline shuddered. "I hope we're not going to start out on those! I don't want to fall."

"I don't think we're going to be jumping at all, at least for a while," Ashleigh said. "We're just going to learn equitation for now."

"Last chance to back out." Caroline sighed. "I think I'd rather be doing my homework."

"Very funny." Ashleigh walked quickly up the lane toward the huge main barn. She was anxious to meet her horse. Also, the indoor ring, where they would have their lesson, was probably there. The large barn was flanked by several smaller stabling barns.

Ashleigh stepped through wide double doors into the immaculate, airy barn and walked down the concrete aisle, admiring the horses. Most of them looked like different kinds of warmbloods, which she knew were often used for dressage and jumping. Ashleigh thought a few horses, the ones with slightly prominent eyes and finely bred, elegant heads, were Thoroughbreds.

The stable was quiet, except for the occasional nicker or stamp of a horse. Ashleigh saw a group of people at the far end of the barn, talking.

"These horses are huge!" Caroline peered into a stall. The black horse inside suddenly popped her head over the door, and Caroline jumped back.

"They're a lot bigger than Moe, that's for sure," Ashleigh said, studying the black horse's muscular shoulders and hindquarters. The mare looked like a jumper. "Most of them are over sixteen hands."

"We'll have to use a mounting block to get on," Caroline said.

"Or jump high." Ashleigh felt excited all over again at

32

the thought of riding one of those beautiful, well-trained horses.

"Are you Ashleigh and Caroline?" someone behind them asked.

Ashleigh turned and saw a dark-haired young woman wearing jeans, scuffed jodhpur boots, and a jean jacket.

"Yes, we are," Caroline answered.

"I'm Jane Stanton, an instructor here." Jane shook hands with them briskly. "You'll be in my equitation class."

Ashleigh stared at Jane. Ashleigh had just recognized her—the previous summer Jane had ridden on the U.S. Olympic steeplechase team. *She's going to be my teacher?* Ashleigh thought. *I can't believe my luck!*

"I've heard of Edgardale," Jane said. "Your farm has some promising stock."

"We hope so," Caroline answered.

"Let's introduce you both to your horses and get started. I'll give you a quick tour on the way. The tack room is there." Jane pointed to a door in the middle of the barn. "The horses' tack is on racks labeled with their names."

"Are all these horses jumpers?" Ashleigh asked as they walked down the aisle.

"Some of them are." Jane pointed to one of the stalls. "This one is my three-day-eventer, Runaround. He's a Thoroughbred."

Ashleigh looked in at the sleek liver chestnut. The horse had long, smooth lines, but the powerful hindquarters of a jumper.

I can't wait to see my school horse, Ashleigh thought as they continued down the aisle. *I hope he's like these horses.*

Jane stopped at a stall near the far end of the barn. "Here's Ranger, Ashleigh. You'll ride him."

Her heart pounding, Ashleigh looked into the stall. A honey-colored chestnut, with a long flaxen mane and tail, stood near the back. "That's my horse?" Ashleigh asked in amazement. "He's gorgeous!"

"He's part Thoroughbred and part Trakehner—that gives him those strong hindquarters," Jane said. "I also use him as a jumping school horse."

Ashleigh opened the stall door and eagerly approached Ranger. "Hi, handsome boy!" she said.

Ranger stretched out his neck a little, but he wasn't too friendly. *Since he's a school horse, he must be used to a lot of riders,* Ashleigh thought. *It'll take a while to make him my special horse.*

"Tack him up and bring him to the indoor ring," Jane said. "It's in this barn, through the doors at the center of the aisle. Caroline, come with me and I'll introduce you to your horse, Neptune."

Ashleigh put Ranger in crossties and went to get his brushes and tack from the tack room. When she returned, Ranger twisted his head around to watch her. He was looking at Ashleigh intelligently. She was used to that kind of look from the Thoroughbreds in her own barn, but there was something else in Ranger's expression.

"What are you thinking?" she asked as she thoroughly brushed him. Ranger's coat was short and glossy because he wore a blanket in the winter. "I guess I'll find out soon enough. But you really are a handsome guy. I think we'll like each other."

Ranger sniffed Ashleigh's fingers. He gave a long, deep sigh and turned away.

"So now you know who I am," Ashleigh said. "This lesson is going to be fun if we both try our best."

Ranger stood docilely while Ashleigh saddled him. *So far, so good,* she thought. She picked up the bridle and tried to pull the headpiece over his nose. Ranger quickly tossed his head aside. Ashleigh tried again. This time Ranger moved his head even faster.

She took a deep breath. "Okay, Ranger. You'd better cooperate, because otherwise—"

Ranger pricked his ears, listening. While he was distracted by her voice, Ashleigh stealthily moved closer with the bridle. Suddenly she pounced and pulled the headpiece up over his nose.

Ranger snorted indignantly. "Now I've got you," Ashleigh said triumphantly. A second later she realized she'd spoken too soon. Ranger refused to open his mouth to take the bit.

Now what? she thought.

Jane looked over the door. "Rest the bit on the palm of your hand and use your thumb to press down on the corner of his mouth," she said. "Keep pressing until he opens up."

Ashleigh tried it, and with very little pressure Ranger opened his mouth. She levered the bit inside and slipped the headpiece over his ears. "You just wanted to see if I was going to make you," Ashleigh said.

"That's right. I guess I forgot to tell you—Ranger's an old pro. He knows every trick in the book," Jane said dryly. "But he can be an excellent horse. He'll perform as well as you make him. Your parents said you're a good rider, so I wanted to try you on him."

"Good," Ashleigh said. "I don't want to ride an easy horse."

For just an instant Ashleigh thought she saw a glimmer of a smile on Jane's stern face. Then it vanished. "Check his saddle," Jane said. It sounded like a warning.

Ashleigh checked the girth and stirrup leathers for wear, then put her fingers under the girth to see if it was tight enough, the way her mother had taught her years earlier with Moe. The saddle seemed fine.

"Okay, boy. This is it!" Ashleigh said happily as she led Ranger into the high-ceilinged indoor ring. On two sides of the ring were bleachers. Walls, gates, and bar jumps were stacked in a corner. Diana and her friends Barbara and Cheryl were already circling the ring on their horses at a walk. Jane stood in the center, frowning as she watched. Caroline was just getting on a tall grey, using a mounting block.

Ashleigh patted Ranger's neck and put her foot in the stirrup to mount. A second later she almost fell over backward. The saddle had slid around until it was hanging almost upside down from Ranger's stomach.

Diana and her friends hooted. "Ride 'em, cowboy," Barbara yelled.

Ashleigh knew her face was burning. *How could I do something so dumb?* she thought.

Jane walked over and pulled the saddle upright again on Ranger's back. "Ranger blows up when he's saddled," she said.

"I just found that out." Ashleigh quickly tightened Ranger's girth by three notches. She didn't want to sound rude, but Jane hadn't exactly told her anything she didn't know. "I'll watch for that the next time I ride," she added, mounting.

Jane nodded. "Good. Okay, walk him around a couple of times and try to get a feel for how he goes. Then move him out in a trot. We're not going to try anything fancy today, although Ranger's capable of it."

Ashleigh forgot her embarrassment about the saddle as she focused on the horse beneath her. Ranger's stride was long and smooth, very unlike Moe's quick steps. Ashleigh half closed her eyes, concentrating on the tension in the reins as she communicated with the new horse.

Diana rode up next to her on her big Dutch warmblood. "Well, look who's here," she said casually.

Ashleigh ignored the comment. "Nice horse," she said. Diana's horse was one of the most beautiful horses Ashleigh had ever seen, whatever his rider was like. He was gray, almost the color of silver, with a darker gray mane and tail.

"This is Silverado." Diana leaned forward and casually ran her hand through Silverado's mane. "You were so late, I didn't think you were going to show up," she added. "I guess you had trouble tacking up the horse."

"No, I *didn't*," Ashleigh said sharply. She was getting tired of Diana's nasty remarks. Across the ring she saw Barbara ride up to Caroline and say something to her.

Diana laughed. "I would have helped you, but I didn't know you were here. We keep our horses in one of the other barns, and the grooms get them ready. The main barn is just for the stable nags."

Ashleigh shrugged. She'd made two circuits of the ring, and Jane had said she wanted them to trot. "Excuse me," Ashleigh said. What signal would cue Ranger perfectly into a trot? She squeezed her legs gradually until she felt the horse break into the faster pace, then sat to the trot. Posting to the trot would have been easier, but at a sitting trot she could feel her horse's every movement. She wanted to get the position of her hands and legs perfect with this horse, so that they moved as a team.

They made several circuits of the ring. After a few minutes Ashleigh thought she had it—her seat was deep and easy in the saddle, and her hands maintained a steady but light pressure on Ranger's mouth, so that he was ready to respond to the slightest signal.

Ashleigh glanced up and saw Jane nod at her.

Good, Ashleigh thought. *I guess that's what she wanted.*

Jane looked over at Caroline. "Caroline, take up your reins and give your horse a little guidance," she yelled. "He's flopping all over the place!"

Ashleigh saw her sister try to follow Jane's instructions, but the harsh words had obviously rattled her. Caroline managed to take up Neptune's reins—but her heels came up, too. She dropped the reins again.

"Caroline, don't sit there like a bag of oats," Jane bellowed. "For the twelfth time, *take up your reins!* Watch Ashleigh!"

Ashleigh saw her sister try to look over, but at that

instant Neptune lunged forward. Caroline gave a little cry and struggled to pull him up. She finally managed to stop him in a corner.

Ashleigh bit her lip. Caroline's face was red, and Ashleigh thought her sister might cry. Caroline was so shaken, Jane seemed to give up on her for the moment.

Poor Caroline, Ashleigh thought. *I hope Jane doesn't start on me.*

"Hands not quite so far forward on Ranger's neck," Jane shouted at Ashleigh, as if she'd read Ashleigh's mind. "And sit back more in the saddle—we're not at the races!"

Ashleigh's concentration wavered from her horse for just a second as she tried to adjust her position. The next second she saw Ranger drop his head. He was going to buck!

Ashleigh checked him sharply with the reins, and Ranger threw up his head with a surprised snort. She wanted to get the message across to Ranger right from the start that he wasn't going to get away with any funny business. Otherwise he'd never quit testing her. She'd never be able to concentrate on improving her riding.

Ashleigh wondered what trick Ranger would try next. Well, she wouldn't let him try any at all. She'd keep a firm hand on the reins and stay alert.

As if he sensed her intentions, Ranger settled into a smooth, extended trot. Ashleigh tried to remember what Jane had told her. She moved her hands into position just over Ranger's withers and settled back in the saddle. Suddenly it all seemed to click, and Ashleigh understood why her position was correct now.

"That's the way to make him mind, Ashleigh!" Jane called. "Everyone please move out in a canter!"

Ashleigh cued Ranger to canter and glanced over at Diana. After Diana's snotty words to her, Ashleigh was curious to see just how good a rider Diana was.

Diana was athletic and moved smoothly with the horse. But it would be hard not to look good on a horse of Silverado's caliber, Ashleigh thought.

"Shoulders back, Diana," Jane corrected. Diana didn't seem to hear her. She certainly didn't change her position. Jane turned back to Ashleigh.

"Try to collect Ranger," Jane instructed. "Tighten your reins and at the same time urge him forward a little. That sounds like a contradiction, but if you do that, he'll be well in hand and look the way he should."

Ashleigh tried it. Ranger's neck arched and his strides became even.

"Exactly," Jane said.

"Good boy," Ashleigh praised. The chestnut gelding's ears flicked back, listening to her. He easily responded to every touch of Ashleigh's legs or hands. Now Ranger wasn't just minding her. They were truly working together.

It's such a wonderful feeling, Ashleigh thought. *Almost like we could take off into the clouds.*

She heard loud giggles across the ring. Ashleigh looked over and saw Diana and Cheryl laughing and untangling their reins. Silverado was shaking his elegant head hard, as if it hurt. Ashleigh realized their horses had just run into each other.

How can they laugh about it? she wondered.

Jane looked furious. "Girls, this is not a joke. Even at slow speeds, a collision between horses can cause serious injury." Jane tapped her boot with her crop. "I think that's enough for today. Cool out your horses if you think they need it."

Ashleigh led Ranger out of the ring. He nudged her playfully with his nose. "We did turn out to be friends," Ashleigh told him, reaching around to rub his forehead. "I guess this wasn't much of a workout for you, was it?"

"We'll step up the pace with you two," Jane said from behind them. She actually smiled, Ashleigh noticed. "See you Saturday." She walked out of the arena ahead of them.

Diana led Silverado up to Ranger. "Trying to suck up to the teacher?" she sneered.

Ashleigh shrugged. "Just learning to ride."

"You could definitely improve at that." Diana had a nasty expression on her face.

"That's what we're supposed to be here for." Ashleigh clucked to Ranger. She'd had enough of Diana's remarks—and this conversation was just going from bad to worse. "Come on, boy, let's put you up. You were so good today!"

Ashleigh crosstied Ranger and went to get his brushes from the tack room. When she got back, Ranger was looking at her quizzically, as if he wasn't quite sure about her yet.

"A good brushing will relax you," she told him. Ashleigh began to brush with the rubber currycomb in long, circular motions. Sure enough, after a few minutes Ranger was leaning into her strokes, with his eyes half closed. When she was done grooming him, Ashleigh put him in his stall. Then she scratched along his neck until she found his favorite spot.

Caroline looked over Ranger's stall door. "I put Neptune up. I'm going out front to see if Mom is here yet. I can't wait to get away from this place—Barbara kept bugging me, and Jane is awful." Ashleigh noticed that Caroline's face was flushed.

"I don't think Jane was trying to be mean," Ashleigh said.

"That's easy for you to say. You could do what she wanted. I was just so embarrassed," Caroline said. "Besides, I didn't want to take up my reins and hurt the horse's mouth."

"You wouldn't have hurt his mouth. Jane wanted you to keep Neptune on a tighter rein so that you could tell him what to do. He needs to feel a slight pressure, or he'll just wander off wherever he wants."

Caroline grimaced. "He certainly did that! I don't know if I'm cut out for riding lessons, Ash."

"Yes, you are," Ashleigh said. But she was wondering the same thing about her sister. So far, Caroline had been afraid of the horse, of getting hurt, and of hurting the horse. Now she was afraid of not doing well enough in the class. "Jane said your seat was satisfactory," Ashleigh pointed out. "That's the only nice thing she said to anybody during the lesson."

"But you should have seen how she was *looking* at you. Like you were a rider sent from heaven." Caroline stepped over to a nearby tap and ran water over her hands. "This is *not* getting me clean. I want to change my clothes, too—these are covered with stable grunge. Are you about ready to go?"

"I'll be ready as soon as I wipe off Ranger's tack." *Funny,* Ashleigh thought as she walked to the tack room. *Caroline wants to get her clothes clean, but I know she didn't clean her horse's tack.*

Ashleigh drew up a folding chair and positioned her saddle in front of her on a sawhorse. She glanced at the many other saddles in the room, gleaming on posts on the wall. "I'll bet every single saddle in here is at least a Crosby," she murmured. "Cool."

Ashleigh carefully wiped down the saddle with liquid saddle soap and a soft cloth. While she was buffing the saddle to a high gloss, she heard voices coming down the aisle.

"Are they gone?" Diana asked.

"I think so. In their rattletrap pickup," Barbara answered.

Ashleigh felt her cheeks grow hot. A lot of people drove pickups, but she was sure Barbara was talking about the Griffens'.

"They were just awful in class," Cheryl said. "Caroline is a total coward."

Ashleigh jumped up angrily. No one was going to say anything mean about Caroline—not while she was around!

"I don't know why Jane thought Ashleigh was so great." Diana laughed, but she didn't sound as if she thought anything was funny. "She looked so silly on that naggy Ranger."

Ashleigh made a face and sat down to her cleaning again. This was dumb. It wasn't anything to get mad about.

"But I really don't want them in the class," Diana went on. Her voice was so firm, Ashleigh wondered if the decision was somehow up to her. "They're taking up all of the teacher's time—Caroline because she's such a bad rider, and Ashleigh because she's just a pain."

"So what are we going to do about them?" Barbara asked.

"I know exactly what," Diana answered. Ashleigh thought Diana sounded much more energetic than she had during the whole riding lesson. "We've got to make them absolutely hate coming to the stable. . . ."

The voices grew fainter as the girls walked down the aisle. Ashleigh hurried to the door of the tack room and looked out.

"We'll . . . Even she won't be able to stand it. . . . And then she won't have anything to ride, not even a stable nag!"

"Great idea!" somebody said. All the girls in the group laughed as they walked out the front double doors of the stable.

Ashleigh took Ranger's bridle down from the hook and polished the bit hard with her cleaning cloth. *They're definitely out to get me,* she thought. *But I won't let them.*

5

"Easy, baby," Ashleigh said to Sunstorm. "We're just going for a walk." It was Wednesday after school, and Ashleigh was gentling Sunstorm officially for the first time. Ashleigh had liked her riding lessons and Jane, but in a way she was glad to get away from the riding stable. She wanted to be around horses, but it was so much less complicated at Edgardale!

The gray colt tossed his head and took a few uncertain steps forward. Ashleigh planned to lead him up and down from the paddock to the stable yard until he effortlessly obeyed her commands.

"This way," Ashleigh urged, pulling on the lead line.

Mrs. Griffen was watching from a few feet away. "Ashleigh, be very careful," she said. "I know you've played with the colt, but schooling him is quite different."

Ashleigh smiled and rubbed Sunstorm's nose. "We're friends. It'll be okay."

"You can't take anything for granted with a young horse—he doesn't know what you want yet," Mrs. Griffen warned. "Older horses will follow you on the lead line. They'll try not to step on you, and they'll stop when you tell them to. But horses aren't born knowing all that. You've got real potential for an injury when a young horse gets confused or scared."

Ashleigh nodded. She knew her mother was right, but Sunstorm was minding beautifully. They made several circuits between the big paddock and the barn.

The six weanlings in the paddock lifted their heads and watched with curiosity. *Sunstorm's training is going so well, I might have time to work them soon, too,* Ashleigh thought.

"I'm going to take him down the driveway," she said to her mother. "The more new things he sees and gets used to, the better he'll behave at the auction."

Mrs. Griffen nodded. "Sounds like a good idea. Just stay alert with him. I'll watch from here for a while."

"Okay. Come on, boy." Ashleigh pulled gently on the line, and Sunstorm followed her down the gravel drive. Ashleigh watched Sunstorm's light, quick steps. He certainly moved with easy grace.

A recent storm had shaken the trees almost bare, and dead leaves rattled at Ashleigh's feet. The sky was still overcast, and the wind was picking up again. Maybe it would storm again, Ashleigh thought.

She realized she was daydreaming and looked quickly at Sunstorm. He was stepping along a pace behind her, exactly the way he should.

He's making such great progress, Ashleigh thought. *Maybe tomorrow we'll try a trot.*

The wind caught an empty paper feed bag. It slowly spiraled toward them. Sunstorm stopped in his tracks and snorted.

"It's just a bag," Ashleigh soothed. "That's what your dinner comes in."

Sunstorm seemed to buy her explanation. They moved forward again. The next second a sudden gust of wind blew the bag right at them. It caught Sunstorm in the head.

With a high, frantic whinny Sunstorm reared, clawing the air with his hooves. Ashleigh narrowly managed to avoid them. The bag dropped to the ground, but it tangled around the colt's legs. Sunstorm furiously sidestepped, trying to get away from it. The next second he bolted.

Ashleigh tightened her grip on the lead line, but she knew she had reacted a second late. Sunstorm was already yanking the line through her hands.

"Try to pull his head around—circle him!" Mrs. Griffen yelled.

Ashleigh dug in her heels and yanked. The muscles stood out on Sunstorm's neck as he fought her. The rapidly moving rope was cutting into Ashleigh's hands, but she hung on anyway.

"Let go of him!" Mrs. Griffen cried. "Don't hurt yourself!"

"No!" Ashleigh couldn't let Sunstorm go. That would send the message to the colt that anytime he wanted, he could pull away from his handler.

But she was fast losing the contest of strength. She still

had a little rope left before the colt would yank the end of it away and be loose. Ashleigh gave it a series of short, sharp tugs.

Caught off balance, Sunstorm lost his forward momentum. He was pulled around almost facing Ashleigh. Suddenly the colt's frightened eyes were looking right into her own.

"Settle down, boy," Ashleigh said through gritted teeth. Finally the colt seemed to understand that the danger was past. His corded muscles relaxed, and he dropped his head. Ashleigh walked toward him, gathering the rope as she went.

As soon as she reached Sunstorm he tucked his head under her arm and rubbed his head against her shirt, as if nothing had happened. "Good, you're acting like a horse again, not a gray tornado," Ashleigh said. She was still trying to catch her breath.

Mrs. Griffen walked down to them. "I didn't think gentling Sunstorm would be so exciting, or I wouldn't have asked you to do it," she said. "But you're doing a great job, honey."

"I almost let him go," Ashleigh said.

"But you didn't. That was a good lesson all around," Mrs. Griffen said. "He learned that he can't get away, and you learned that you have to watch him every second. I think he knows now that he can trust you, too. He found out the danger wasn't anything, which was what you were trying to tell him."

"He learned I'll protect him from feed bags." Ashleigh laughed.

"I think he'll go well for you from now on." Mrs. Griffen picked up Ashleigh's free hand. The rope had seared a deep red mark on the skin and cut it in places. "We need to bandage you up. Then I'll take him around, just for today."

"My hand doesn't hurt. I'll bandage it later." Ashleigh led Sunstorm forward again. "I can keep working him. I want to show him that feed bag close up. And *then* we're going to walk down the driveway, like I told him we would. He's going to mind."

The Saturday of the Breeders' Cup races dawned unseasonably cold, even for early November. As Ashleigh walked with her family onto the backside at Churchill Downs, she noticed that the sky was a flat, uniform gray.

The weather's fine as long as it doesn't rain, she thought.

Caroline pulled her hat over her ears. "It's freezing!" she said.

"Almost snowing," Rory agreed.

"Don't be wimps," said Mr. Griffen. "It's not that cold."

Ashleigh was much too excited and happy to be cold. Her riding lesson that day had been canceled, since Jane would be at the Breeders' Cup. Half the people in Kentucky were there to see the rich, prestigious races.

On the backside, champion Thoroughbreds were being groomed, walked, and bandaged in preparation for their races. Most of the horses seemed calmer than their owners and trainers.

"There's Triple Derby!" Ashleigh said. The tall black stallion was walking with his groom to the shed row. He seemed full of himself, as usual—he was half dragging the groom, who kept a firm grip on his halter.

"Let's introduce ourselves to his owners," Mrs. Griffen said. "After all, we own Triple Derby's half-sister. That makes us practically related."

"Besides, Triple Derby isn't owned by one of the big stables. Those people might not want to fraternize with a smaller breeder," Mr. Griffen said. "He belongs to Nick Blair, who is an architect. Bob bought the colt for a very low price at auction, considering what he's done since."

As the Griffens walked to Triple Derby's shed row, a gorgeous horse, flanked by his groom, trainer, and owner, crossed directly in front of them. Ashleigh studied the horse carefully. Even among so many exquisite horses, she could tell that this one was special. He was a big liver chestnut, with a glittering dark coat and bright, intelligent eyes. He had a narrow white blaze ending in a perfectly shaped star on his forehead.

"Who's that?" Ashleigh asked.

"That's Rambunctious," Mr. Griffen said. "The Kentucky Derby winner."

Ashleigh drew a deep breath. "Wow," she said.

"Wow is right," Mrs. Griffen agreed. "He's favored to win the Classic today over Triple Derby. Triple Derby's had a good year, but lately there have been some questions about his soundness. He placed fifth in his last stakes race."

In front of Triple Derby's stall a heavyset man sat in a

folding chair. "Hi, folks," he said. "What can I do for you?"

"We're Zip Away's owners." Mr. Griffen introduced them all. "We own Griffen Breeding Farm."

"I'm Bob Taylor, Triple's trainer." Mr. Taylor tipped his hat. "Never heard of your farm, but I've heard of Zip Away. Do you have any foals out of her?"

"Just one—Sunstorm, by Sunflyer."

"That's an unusual cross," Bob Taylor said. "Sunflyer's line is prone to unsoundness. How's the colt doing?"

"Great," Ashleigh said quickly.

Mr. Taylor laughed. "Are you his trainer, young lady?"

Ashleigh frowned. "No," she said.

"Ashleigh's been working with the colt," Mrs. Griffen said. "Of course it's early days yet, but we haven't had any problems with soundness. He's a good-looking horse, too, like his uncle. I think he'll make an impression at the January auction."

Bob Taylor pushed back his hat. "It might make sense to wait to auction him. The auctions later in the year usually bring higher prices. If Triple wins the Classic today, for the second year in a row, you'll have yourself a valuable colt."

"We'll be cheering for Triple Derby," Caroline said.

"So are you going to wait for the July or September auction to sell Sunstorm?" Ashleigh asked her parents eagerly as they walked to their seats. That would be great news—she and Sunstorm would be together a lot longer!

"I don't think so, sweetie." Mrs. Griffen shook her head. "Our financial needs are fairly pressing."

51

Ashleigh sighed. *I guess I knew that,* she thought.

The nine other Breeders' Cup races would be run before the Classic. Although she knew the horses only by name, Ashleigh picked favorites to root for in every race. By post time for the Classic, Ashleigh had almost lost her voice from cheering.

"Let's get something to eat before the race starts," she suggested to Rory. She asked everybody in her family what they wanted.

At the snack bar she and Rory loaded up on nachos, hot dogs, and sodas. On their way back to the stands the clouds opened up. Ashleigh pulled her slicker over her head to keep out the pelting rain.

As they took their seats and passed around the food, the horses emerged from the tunnel under the stands for the post parade.

"There goes Triple Derby," Ashleigh said excitedly. The tall black horse was walking out onto the track with an escort pony.

"He's coming into this race off a couple of wins at Belmont this summer, even though he lost his last race," Mrs. Griffen said. "Rambunctious is definitely a horse to watch, too. He won the Travers at Saratoga in August."

Ashleigh opened her parents' *Daily Racing Form* and flipped to the page for the Classic. According to the listings, Triple Derby seemed to do well only on fast tracks.

As suddenly as it had begun, the rain stopped. But the track was now listed as sloppy.

Ashleigh watched tensely as the ten Thoroughbreds

were loaded into the gate. Satin Times, a rangy gray from Ireland, balked and had to be pushed in. Triple Derby seemed to be standing a little sideways in the gate, she noticed with concern. Sometimes the horses lost their concentration when there was a delay in the starting gate.

The bell clanged loudly. The horses broke from the gate, an almost solid ball of muscle and power. As they rounded the first turn the field began to stretch out. Triple Derby was in the lead!

"At the quarter mile Triple Derby is setting the early pace," the announcer called.

"He's setting faster fractions than last year's winner," Mr. Griffen said excitedly.

"They're trying to burn him out!" Mrs. Griffen said. She shook her head. "No horse can keep up that pace over a mile."

Triple Derby's jockey clearly thought so, too. He checked Triple Derby until he had him rated fourth down the backstretch behind the pacesetters. The four lead horses maintained their field position around the far turn and coming into the stretch.

"It's time for Triple Derby to make his move," Mr. Griffen said.

"But he's blocked by those three horses in front!" Ashleigh leaned forward.

Triple Derby's jockey checked him again. The jockey would have to take his horse three wide around the front-runners.

"He's hard rating Triple," Mrs. Griffen said. "He's dropping way back."

"No! That's not the way to do it," Ashleigh muttered. "Check him hard just once. He'll get the message. Then try to take him around."

"How do you know that will work?" Caroline turned to look at her in surprise.

"Because that's what I did with Sunstorm." Suddenly Ashleigh gasped. Triple Derby had seized the bit and lunged forward. He was headed straight for a three-wide wall of horses!

"There's nowhere for him to go!" Ashleigh frantically scanned the field. Then she saw that on the inside was a small opening. The jockey gave Triple Derby a short, hard check. At the same time he pointed him at the opening.

Triple Derby roared through. An instant later Satin Times tried to follow. But Rambunctious had moved over, closing the hole. Satin Times's shoulder bumped Rambunctious. The force of the blow knocked the gray colt almost into the rail. Rambunctious staggered but galloped on.

"Satin Times has been savaged," the announcer cried.

But now Triple Derby had the chance to show his speed. The big black stallion changed leads and powered on, heading for the wire. He crossed the finish two lengths ahead of his challengers.

"Hurray!" Ashleigh cheered. This was almost as good as Sunstorm's winning the race—and she was sure he would in two years.

"A great race," Mr. Griffen said as they left the stands and walked to the truck.

"Triple Derby's jockey almost lost the race when he checked him too hard going into the far turn. If I'd been riding, I would have known not to do that," Ashleigh said.

Her parents laughed. "Ashleigh, that's easy for you to say. You were sitting in the grandstand," Mrs. Griffen said. "It's different when you're thundering down a racetrack, with only split seconds to make decisions. And you'd better make the right decision. If you make a mistake, you may well be crushed by a field of thousand-pound horses."

"I guess." Ashleigh frowned.

She lagged behind her parents as they walked to the truck. Behind them she could hear the fainter and fainter whinnies of horses, the blare of announcements, and other sounds from the track.

Rory dropped back to walk with her. "I think you would have ridden Triple Derby better," he said.

Ashleigh smiled. "I think I would have, too."

On Tuesday in school Mr. Gates passed back the science papers. Ashleigh's paper was on the genetics of different coat colors in horses. She had become very interested in the subject and hoped she'd done well. She looked quickly at the grade.

"What did you get?" Mona whispered from her seat across the aisle.

Ashleigh held up the paper.

"Wow, an A!" Mona said. "I got a B-plus."

Diana sat in front of Ashleigh, to her right. Diana didn't turn around, but Ashleigh could tell from the tilt of Diana's head that she was listening to the conversation.

"May I get a drink, Mr. Gates?" Diana asked.

"If you don't talk to anyone on the way." Mr. Gates frowned at her from his desk at the front of the room.

"I won't." Diana jumped up. Her hand knocked her science paper to the floor. It floated down to rest right by Ashleigh's foot.

Without thinking, Ashleigh picked it up and looked at it. The paper was covered with red ink, and the teacher had written "Careless—D" in big letters across the top page.

Diana's face reddened. "Snoop," she said, snatching the paper.

It figures she doesn't care about her schoolwork, Ashleigh thought. *She doesn't care about her riding, either.* "Sorry," she said.

Diana looked mad, but also embarrassed. She glared and slammed the paper facedown on her desk.

After Diana returned from the water fountain, Ashleigh heard whispering. She glanced up and saw Diana, Barbara, and Cheryl with their heads together. After a moment Barbara looked up and gave Ashleigh a hard stare.

"Girls, please get back to work," Mr. Gates said. "Or have you already solved the five sample problems?"

Diana, Barbara, and Cheryl bent over their work. A minute later they all looked up and glared at Ashleigh again.

"They really are out to get me," Ashleigh told Mona as they walked to the bus after school. "I don't care what they say, but I just wonder what they'll do."

"I've never seen Diana act like that," Mona said. "She didn't used to be mean."

"I know." Ashleigh shifted her books to squeeze through a crowd of kids. "But she's been acting so weird, I think I'd better check my tack before the lesson to make sure it's not cut or something like that."

"That would be a terrible thing to do." Mona looked shocked.

"Yeah, but Diana hates me for doing better than she does in the riding class. She might even still be upset about soccer tryouts last year. And now she's mad about the science paper."

"None of that is your fault," Mona said.

"I know. But Diana thinks it is." Ashleigh stopped for a moment on the steps of the bus. "I don't know how far she'll go to get even."

6

ASHLEIGH WALKED INTO RANGER'S STALL THAT AFTERNOON and groaned. "Oh, no. Look at you!" She could hardly believe her eyes. The riding lesson started in just ten minutes—and Ranger was caked from nose to tail with an inch of manure.

Diana and her gang had done such a thorough job, Ashleigh almost had to admire it. Even Ranger's eyelids were coated.

"All right, boy, let's get to work on you," she said. "But believe me, I'll get them back for this." Ranger swung his head around to nudge her affectionately. The dried manure on his neck cracked. Ashleigh groaned again.

In the tack room she looked for Ranger's wire currycomb in his grooming box. That was the only brush that made any headway against dried mud or, she hoped, dried manure. The currycomb had disappeared.

"Now what?" she said aloud. "I guess since Diana stole Ranger's curry, I should take Silverado's." Diana's large, fancy tack trunk was in plain view on the floor. But when Ashleigh tried to open it, she found it was locked. Finally Ashleigh dug into Neptune's box and borrowed his spare.

Ranger stuck his head out over the stall door, looking to see where she was. Ashleigh almost laughed. Ranger's eyes were very dark in contrast to his new, paler coat, and wisps of straw clung to his mane.

"I guess you do well at whatever you like," Ashleigh said to him, letting herself into the stall. "And manuring horses must be what Diana likes to do. I just hope she's done getting even with me now—for soccer, and the science grade, and my riding better than she does. I don't know. That does sound like kind of a lot."

Ranger yawned and rubbed his dirty ears against her shirt. *At least he seems perfectly happy,* Ashleigh thought. *Probably he likes all the attention.*

Half an hour later, Ashleigh was satisfied that no traces of Diana's work were left on Ranger's coat. She looked down at what had been a clean T-shirt and breeches. "I'm sort of a mess," she said.

Ranger snorted and shook his head.

"I know, it would have been fine with you if we'd just gone out the way you were," Ashleigh said. "Maybe that's what I should have done—then when Jane saw what you looked like, Diana would have been in trouble instead of us."

"You're late," Jane snapped when Ashleigh led Ranger into the ring.

"Sorry, Jane." Ashleigh quickly mounted. She was even later than she'd expected to be when she first saw Ranger's coat of manure, because Diana and her friends had also poured neat's-foot oil all over his saddle. Ashleigh had to spend another ten minutes mopping it off.

All the other horses and riders were posting to the trot around the ring. Ashleigh saw Diana laugh and pull her horse closer to Barbara's.

"Straighten up, Diana and Barbara," Jane called. "And keep your distance. This isn't a polo class."

Diana and Barbara separated. Barbara guided her bay gelding, Shoo-in, around the other horses to catch up to Ashleigh.

"Something smells," Barbara said when she was within earshot.

"Must be the stinky people with dumb ideas," Ashleigh said sweetly.

Barbara frowned.

"The manure made Ranger look sort of nice," Ashleigh said casually. "It turned him into a dun—I've always liked that color."

"You've got to be kidding." Barbara stared at her in disgust. "But it figures that you'd like a manure horse. That's probably the best you can afford."

"I've got *seventeen* horses of my own," Ashleigh said. "All of them are registered Thoroughbreds." *Let her try to top that,* she thought with satisfaction.

"Yeah, third-rate claimers." Barbara snorted. "We all know where you buy your horses."

Ashleigh shrugged. A secret smile curved her lips. *Barbara wouldn't criticize if she could see our beautiful horses!*

Barbara made a face. Ashleigh noticed that she and Diana were riding right behind her.

"Posting trot, everyone!" Jane called.

Ashleigh put her mind on her riding. In the first lesson she felt that she and Ranger had clicked. Now she wanted to work on the fine points of balance and position so that she could look as good as possible. She'd read in one of her horse books the night before that her fingers should be curled around the reins with the little finger on the outside and the thumbs up, at about a forty-five-degree angle. Her legs should press back against the saddle flaps and be slightly open at the knee.

Ranger's mind, though, seemed elsewhere. He refused to move out smoothly at the trot. Ashleigh had to keep urging him forward with her legs and hands. It was hard to practice anything difficult. *I wonder if Diana asked you to act up,* Ashleigh thought. *I really, really wish I had my own horse.*

Caroline rode up next to her on Neptune. "What happened?" she asked. "You took so long to get out here."

"Nothing," Ashleigh said absently, moving her hands back a notch over Ranger's withers. Yes—that position both improved her balance and was more comfortable. "I'll tell you later," she added.

"Ashleigh, I think you put too much oil on that saddle—you're sitting in a pool of grease," Jane remarked.

Diana and her friends shrieked with laughter. "Look at her bottom," Barbara gasped.

"I like my saddle well oiled," Ashleigh said, twisting around in the saddle to face Barbara. "It helps me move in it. You don't think my perfect seat is just by accident, do you?"

"You don't have a perfect seat," Diana snapped.

"Yes, she does," Jane said unexpectedly. "Okay, everybody walk. Ashleigh, please ride around the ring, first sitting, then posting to the trot. I want to point out what you're doing right to the class."

Caroline grinned and gave Ashleigh a thumbs-up sign.

Ashleigh moved Ranger out at a trot. The chestnut gelding easily picked up the quicker pace, arching his neck and lifting his feet lightly. He'd settled down, Ashleigh noted. *Maybe I was kind of nervous at first,* she thought. *He might have just been picking up on that.*

"Notice first how relaxed Ashleigh is," Jane began. "Ranger is relaxed, too, and moving out freely, but through the correct tension in the reins Ashleigh has him well in hand. He's ready for her signals. Caroline, that's why you need to have your reins tighter. The horse won't object—he expects contact with his mouth. Walk Ranger for a minute, please, Ashleigh. Then put him back into the trot."

This is easy, Ashleigh thought. She put Ranger back in the trot with the merest pressure of her legs. Ranger trotted effortlessly, his powerful muscles bunching and releasing. Ashleigh wondered what it would be like to jump him.

"Diana, you lean forward too much and sometimes

curve over. That doesn't look good, and it puts your balance off in cuing the horse. Excellent, Ashleigh."

"Way to go, Ash!" Caroline said. Barbara snorted.

"All right, everybody. Remember, it's just about a month to our annual Christmas show," Jane said. "Ashleigh and Caroline, you're welcome to participate if you think you're ready. We're having the show early in December since some of you mentioned to me you have vacation plans over the holidays."

"We're going to Barbados again this year," Diana said, as if it was no big deal.

"I'm going to the end of my driveway and back to the barn again this year," Caroline said in exactly the same tone Diana had used.

"In our rattletrap pickup," Ashleigh added.

"Girls!" Jane clapped sharply. "That's enough. Let's get to work. Diana, we don't have much time before the show to get the curve out of your back. Thanks for the demonstration, Ashleigh. Ranger's doing very well these days." She smiled.

"Thanks," Ashleigh said. "I'd love to be in the Christmas show." She started to smile back at Jane. Then Ashleigh saw the look on Diana's face.

I wonder what dirty tricks Diana will try next, she thought with a sigh.

"Sit up straighter, Rory!" Ashleigh urged. She was standing in the center of the stable yard at Edgardale a week later, watching Rory circle on Moe. She was giving him his first riding lesson. It was almost Thanksgiving.

She'd have time to give him a lot more coaching during the Thanksgiving vacation, when they didn't have school.

"I can't sit up straight—Moe's round!" Rory called back. He was hanging on to the pommel of the saddle with one hand and Moe's mane with the other. Somewhere in between, the reins were all tangled up.

Ashleigh tried not to laugh. She knew she shouldn't. She was Rory's riding instructor, and Jane certainly never laughed during a lesson. Ashleigh assumed a stern expression.

Being a riding instructor isn't bad, especially on a day like this, Ashleigh decided. The previous night had been the coldest yet of the year, and spiderwebs of frost crisscrossed the ground in front of the barn. But the sun was bright, spilling yellow light on the stable yard and drive. It seemed so easy to see that day—out to the horses in the paddocks, their coats gleaming like fire, and beyond to the gray-black woods.

Ashleigh inhaled a deep breath of the clear, cold air and walked over to Rory. "Hold up a minute." Moe saw her coming and stopped dead. Probably he hoped it was time to go back to the paddock.

"Moe's acting weird," Rory complained.

"No, he isn't. He just doesn't know what you want him to do." Ashleigh expertly untangled the reins and put them correctly into Rory's small hands. Then she pushed Rory up straight in the saddle. "Now try again. Don't hang on to his mane or the saddle, or you won't be able to control him. You have to balance and use the reins."

"This is hard," Rory said.

"Don't give up. You won't become the world's greatest rider in a day." Ashleigh stepped back and watched critically as Rory urged Moe around the yard again.

She was surprised how hard it was to teach Rory. Most of what Ashleigh knew about riding was instinctive—the exact tension she should feel in the reins, how hard to squeeze with her legs. And what her hands and legs were doing changed slightly with the horse's response to her cues and its every movement.

Suddenly Moe broke into a trot.

"I-I-I can't . . . do this!" Rory yelled. "M-My teeth are falling out!"

"Go with him, Rory!" Ashleigh said. "Don't tense up. Relax and follow his movements. But hang on tight!" *I don't think I said that very well,* she thought ruefully.

Rory almost fell off to the left. Ashleigh rushed to try to prop him up, but by that time he was leaning to the right. Rory began to giggle as Ashleigh ran around to that side.

"Don't sit there and laugh, Rory!" Ashleigh said. She was getting out of breath. "Either pull him up or do it right!"

Rory's brow furrowed with concentration. Then, to Ashleigh's surprise, he suddenly seemed to figure it out. His posture was good, and his seat wasn't lopsided.

"Look, Ashleigh!" he said triumphantly. "We're doing great!"

"Yes, you are." Ashleigh stepped back to the center of the yard to watch. She felt a pang at how perfectly Moe and Rory fit together. That was the way she and Moe used to look.

Mrs. Griffen mounted Gallantry in front of the barn and trotted the mare past them.

"Hey, Mom, look at Rory!" Ashleigh called.

With difficulty Mrs. Griffen reined Gallantry in. The dark bay mare strained against the pressure of the bit, dancing in place.

"That's wonderful, sweetie!" Mrs. Griffen said. Ashleigh noticed that her mother took her eyes off Gallantry for barely a second.

"How come you're riding her?" Ashleigh asked. Her mom didn't look as though she was having a very good time. Gallantry didn't seem too happy, either. Her neck was already dark with sweat.

"With my office job, I'm not in shape to be a jockey," Mrs. Griffen panted. "But this horse needs some real exercise. She's going crazy in the stall. I'm almost tempted to blanket her and leave her out at night—that was your father's idea, since he's the one who has to fix her stall every time she tears it apart. But I'm afraid she'll go through the paddock fence."

"Or over it," Ashleigh murmured. She couldn't stop looking at Gallantry. The fiercely spirited Thoroughbred was so different from Moe or the riding-school horses. The wild, elegant beauty of her action was very unlike the quiet finesse of the trained jumper or the perfectly controlled movements of the dressage horse.

Gallantry threw up her head, dragging the reins through Mrs. Griffen's hands. Then she lunged forward.

Mrs. Griffen hauled on the reins and managed to stop her.

"We'll breed her in February—that may settle her down," Mrs. Griffen said. "In the meantime, since I have to exercise her, I might as well try to teach her some manners."

Ashleigh thought that Gallantry had manners—it was just that they were for the racetrack. The mare clearly had no patience for her role as a pleasure horse.

Rory guided Moe over to Ashleigh. "I want to ride Moe forever," he declared solemnly.

"Then which one will Ashleigh ride?" Mrs. Griffen asked.

"I'll ride Gallantry," Ashleigh offered.

Her mother looked surprised, then shook her head. "This is way too much horse for you. I don't want you overmounted. Believe me, riding a horse you can't handle is one of the scariest experiences there is."

"I could do it," Ashleigh said. She knew she could, if her mother would just let her try. "Jane says if I can ride Ranger, I can ride anything," she added. "He knows every trick in the book."

Her mother laughed. "Sweetie, riding Moe and school horses isn't the same as riding a Thoroughbred racehorse. Even though we've stopped racing Gallantry, she doesn't know that. I'm glad we're not trying to recondition her as a pleasure horse, because I don't think it would work. I'm going to have my hands full just trying to exercise her."

Mrs. Griffen trotted Gallantry out of the stable yard. Gallantry was fighting for her head every inch of the way.

Ashleigh stared after her mother in frustration. She thought she was ready to ride a Thoroughbred—if someone would just give her a chance.

"Ashleigh, look what I can make Moe do!" Rory was circling the pony at a trot.

Ashleigh smiled at her little brother. "Way to go, Rory!" she said. *I can't really be sad about outgrowing Moe when he's making Rory so happy*, she thought. *And soon I'll be moving up in the horse world, too.*

7

MR. GRIFFEN CARRIED IN A STEAMING PLATTER OF SLICED turkey and set it on the dining room table. "Happy Thanksgiving!" he said. "Is anyone hungry?"

"I am!" Rory said eagerly.

"I am, too." Ashleigh had worked up an appetite. She'd gone for a long ride that afternoon under the pale yellow, low-hanging sun, enjoying the sweet scent of the fallen leaves as they crunched under Moe's hooves. She could still feel the glow from the cold on her face.

Mrs. Griffen and Caroline brought in bowls of mashed potatoes, dressing, and salad. Ashleigh lit the candles. The table was laid with the fine Irish lace cloth they used only for special occasions. Mrs. Griffen had inherited it from her grandmother. Ashleigh had set the table with the ornate hundred-year-old silverware that had belonged to her father's mother.

"A toast." Mr. Griffen held up a glass of sparkling water. "To our farm and our family—may we always be as happy and blessed as we are this day."

Ashleigh looked around at her family in the candlelight as they all clinked glasses. Her parents were smiling. Caroline looked pretty and grown-up in a light gray sweater dress, adorned with a string of pearls. Rory's eyes were shining.

Ashleigh took a big forkful of turkey. She loved the warmth of the delicious Thanksgiving meal with her family. Also, Thanksgiving turkey meant that Christmas was just around the corner.

"Today I spoke with Jane," Mrs. Griffen said as they passed around the serving bowls.

"How come?" Ashleigh asked.

"She and I got to talking about the care of horses in a stable over the holidays—she's almost always short-staffed then. I said that over Christmas we could board Ranger and Neptune for two weeks."

Ashleigh stopped eating. "Mom, that's fantastic! I can't believe what a great vacation I'm going to have."

"We'll pick them up just before Christmas at the stable," Mrs. Griffen said. "By the way, Jane was very complimentary about both of you."

Caroline made a face. "About Ashleigh, anyway."

"About you too, Caroline," Mrs. Griffen said. "Jane said you try very hard."

Ashleigh set down her fork. She was much too excited to eat.

"We'll have so much fun, Ash!" Caroline grinned. "I

think I'll like riding a lot better when Jane's not staring at me and criticizing!"

"You bet!" Ashleigh was already planning the rides they would take.

After they had finished eating the main course, Mrs. Griffen brought in from the kitchen two glistening, luscious-looking pumpkin pies.

"Wow!" Rory said. "I could eat one of those all by myself!"

"They really are beautiful," Caroline said. "Good job, Mom."

"Thank you." Mrs. Griffen looked around at the expectant faces. "Ice cream on your pie, anyone?"

As she devoured the delicious dessert Ashleigh thought about what she would do after dinner. The horses deserved a Thanksgiving treat. She'd decided to give them all a handful of sweet feed and an ear scratch. Ashleigh had considered giving everybody a brushing, but to get through seventeen horses and Moe before bedtime she would have had to start that morning.

She also wanted to pick out stalls for Ranger and Neptune. She'd stable them next to each other, since they were used to each other. That way they wouldn't fret.

"Volunteers to help wash up?" Mrs. Griffen called when they had finished the last bite of pie.

"We'll all help." Mr. Griffen started to stack the dishes.

Just as Ashleigh was closing the dishwasher door on a full load, the phone rang. "It's for you, Ash," Caroline called a moment later. Ashleigh took the phone from her sister and carried it into the hall. "Hello?"

"Ashleigh, you have to come over quick!" Mona said.

"Why?" Ashleigh had never heard her friend sound so excited. "What happened?"

"You're never going to believe this—my parents got me a horse!"

"Really?" Ashleigh said slowly. "That's super." *Of course I'm glad for Mona,* she told herself. *But why couldn't it be me?*

"She's a Thoroughbred!"

Ashleigh sucked in a breath. For a few seconds she couldn't say anything. There was almost too much emotion swirling inside for her to know how she felt. "Wow" was all she finally said.

"Can you come over?" Mona asked.

"It's so late—I wouldn't want to see her in the dark," Ashleigh said. "Why don't I ride Moe over tomorrow?"

"Sure," Mona said. "We'll be waiting!"

Ashleigh hung up the phone, feeling a surge of jealousy and disappointment. She realized she hadn't even told Mona her news about boarding Ranger and Neptune at Edgardale over the holidays. But now it didn't seem like much, compared to having your own horse forever.

Mr. Griffen came out into the hall. "Was that Mona?" he asked.

"Yeah. Hey, Dad, guess what? Mona's parents just got her a Thoroughbred," Ashleigh said. "And—"

Mr. Griffen shook his head. "I know what you're going to say next, Ashleigh. But the farm isn't doing well enough yet for us to afford a pleasure horse. You just have to be patient."

72

Ashleigh didn't trust herself to speak. She turned and climbed the stairs to her room. Then she flopped onto the bed and stared at the dark ceiling.

I've been patient, she thought. *And all that's happened is I still don't have a horse!*

The next afternoon Ashleigh rode Moe over to the Gardners' to see Mona's new horse. The whole ride over, Ashleigh forced herself to think of cheerful, positive things to say to Mona. She wasn't going to act the least bit envious, she had decided. She didn't want to take anything away from Mona—she just wanted the same thing herself.

In the Gardners' stable yard she saw Mona, expertly riding a sleek, tall horse with the unmistakable, beautiful lines of a registered Thoroughbred. The horse was a light bay, with a thick, long black mane and tail.

I should just go back home, Ashleigh thought, turning Moe. *I'm not going to be able to handle this.*

"Ashleigh! Over here!" Mona called.

Ashleigh reluctantly rode over to the fence.

"I named her Frisky," Mona said. "See how she jumps around? Isn't she just gorgeous?"

"Yeah. Good name." Ashleigh tried to sound nice. After all, it wasn't Mona's fault that Ashleigh didn't have a horse.

"Watch this." Mona cantered around the yard a couple of times and jumped a cavalletti. Ashleigh almost told her not to show off so much. At last Mona rode up to the fence again.

"That was good," Ashleigh said.

"Frisky's trainer will be coming over once a week to coach us," Mona said.

A stab of pure, solid envy pierced Ashleigh's heart. She tried to control it, but she couldn't. Why did Mona get everything Ashleigh had ever hoped for?

Ashleigh sighed. Maybe she could at least share Frisky with Mona. She might feel better if she got a ride on a Thoroughbred every now and then. "Can I ride her?" Ashleigh asked. She was already getting off Moe.

Mona hesitated. "I don't think so. My trainer said it's better if no one rides her but me. Having more than one rider might mess her up."

"What?" Ashleigh couldn't believe her ears. How could her best friend just stand there calmly saying that Ashleigh would ruin her horse if she rode it?

Mona looked uncomfortable. "I'm sorry, but that's what he told me. Frisky's so highly trained. . . ."

"I won't touch her," Ashleigh said, mounting Moe. "I won't even look at her!"

"Ashleigh!" Mona called, but Ashleigh was already cantering away.

I can't believe she acted like that, Ashleigh thought as she and Moe thundered down the lane to Edgardale. *Well, it's not as if I don't have better things to do. Mona can just stay and be snobby with her horse all by herself.* Ashleigh tried to control her tears.

Back at Edgardale, Ashleigh untacked Moe and let him loose in the paddock. The little pony hesitated by the gate for a second, looking at her.

"It's okay," Ashleigh said. "I'm sorry we didn't have a very good time. But I'll make it up to you soon. Right now I need to work with Sunstorm—we've got only about six weeks until the auction."

Sunstorm walked over from the other weanlings and nudged her. "You're right—let's do something," she said to him.

Ashleigh ran up to the barn and grabbed a halter. When she got back to the paddock, Sunstorm was cantering around, throwing little bucks. The weeks of conditioning were paying off. Sunstorm was sleeker, more muscular, and more beautiful every day.

"Let's do something a little different," she said, buckling on the halter. "Instead of walking or trotting, you just stand, and I'll pick up your feet."

Ashleigh dropped the lead line to the ground. Sunstorm had learned that she didn't want him to run off during lessons. Besides, she didn't want to tie him in case he got upset when she handled his feet. He might injure his head yanking on a tied rope.

Ashleigh decided to try picking up a back leg first. More of horses' weight was on their front feet, and so they usually preferred to pick up the back ones. The only problem with lifting a back foot, Ashleigh knew, was the possibility that she'd get kicked.

She positioned herself to the side of Sunstorm's right back leg, as close to him as possible. That way if he kicked, he wouldn't be able to extend his leg much, and the kick wouldn't be as hard.

"I can't believe you would really kick me," she said.

"But you did try that one day with Moe. And a kick from a horse your size wouldn't feel great."

Ashleigh wanted to get Sunstorm used to having his feet handled. Otherwise, every time he needed shoeing the horseshoer might have to throw him and tie him. She also wanted to break him of the habit of kicking when someone or another horse was behind him.

Very slowly, Ashleigh applied upward pressure on Sunstorm's leg with both hands. At the same time she leaned gently against him, signaling him to take the weight off that foot.

Sunstorm shifted his weight and lifted his foot a little. Then he put it back down and looked around. Ashleigh laughed at the puzzled expression on his face. "I know what I'm doing," she said. "Trust me."

This time the colt let her lift his leg and hold it for a few seconds. Ashleigh went on to his other hind leg. Sunstorm understood what she wanted and easily picked up his foot.

"Great, boy!" Ashleigh praised. "Now let's try a front one."

Ashleigh became totally absorbed in working with Sunstorm. She lifted his front feet and rubbed all his legs. Then she rubbed his tail, back, and sides. Ashleigh felt herself relaxing along with the colt.

By the time she got to his head and was rubbing his forehead, the evening cold was creeping into the air. In a few minutes Ashleigh's parents would come out to bring in the horses.

Sunstorm's shiny gray coat was almost blue in the

fading light. The big colt leaned against her, relishing the caresses. Ashleigh looked out at the paddocks, where the mares, now big with foal, quietly grazed. In the next paddock the tall, elegant weanlings frolicked, nipping each other and kicking up their heels. How could she be jealous of Mona or anybody else when she had all this?

Sunstorm whickered softly. "I was rotten to Mona, wasn't I, boy?" Ashleigh said. "I should have been glad for her, but I spoiled things. Besides, she's never acted jealous of me. And look at what I've got."

A bright rectangle of yellow light appeared as Mr. and Mrs. Griffen opened the front door of the house and came outside to bring in the horses.

"I'd better put you up and go help them," Ashleigh said. "Then I think I owe Mona an apology."

Sunstorm followed her eagerly to the barn. He almost ran into his stall. Ashleigh fed him, lingering at his stall to watch the young horse enjoying his dinner. Then she went out to get the other horses.

The sun had sunk to a cold red glow on the winter horizon. Ashleigh collected Zip Away and Go Gen to take up to the barn. Leading two horses at once took some skill, but Ashleigh had long ago learned to manage it. The trick was to move them quickly, before they had time to think about nipping each other, and keep a firm hold on each.

Soon the barn was filled with the warm breaths and clacking hooves of seventeen horses. All the horses went quietly to their stalls except for Gallantry, who threw up her head and almost lifted Mrs. Griffen off the ground.

Finally the last stall door was shut and the only sound was of contented munching.

Ashleigh went down to the barn office and sat in her dad's chair to call Mona. It was hard for Ashleigh to admit that she'd acted so badly, but she really wanted to apologize to her best friend.

Mona answered on the second ring. "It's me," Ashleigh said. "I'm sorry I got mad. I really do think it's great you got a horse."

"No, I'm sorry," Mona said. "I should have realized how you'd feel. Of course you can ride Frisky sometimes. My trainer probably just meant not to let people who are inexperienced ride her."

"Thanks." Ashleigh was silent a moment. "But can we still ride together? I'm not sure Moe can keep up with Frisky."

"I can always take Toby if he can't," Mona offered. "I'm not giving him away."

"Deal. See you tomorrow."

"Sounds good."

Ashleigh hung up and walked back down the barn aisle. She was glad she and Mona had made up. Ashleigh didn't want to ever fight with her best friend, not even over a horse.

8

ASHLEIGH ARRIVED EARLY AT CHESTERTON ON THE DAY OF
the Christmas show. She had a lot to do to get Ranger
ready. Jane had said she'd braid the horses' manes and
tails that morning. But Ashleigh still needed to oil
Ranger's hooves, polish his tack, and give him the
brushing of his life. She wanted his beautiful chestnut coat
to be as shiny as possible.

Ranger had recognized her steps and was hanging his
head out over the half-door of his stall. He tossed his head
and gave her a welcoming nicker as she approached.

Ashleigh looked at him, her eyes widening in shock.
The manure had been bad enough. She couldn't believe
what she saw now. Ranger was covered with red, green,
and white glitter. Even in the subdued light of the barn,
thousands of little spangles flashed every time he moved.

Ashleigh swallowed hard. It would be incredibly hard
to get off all that glitter. "What am I going to do?" she

murmured. "I can't give you a bath when it's thirty degrees out. And we've only got two hours till the show starts—that's not enough time to pick it all off."

Ranger looked at her alertly, as if he was awaiting her decision. He didn't look half bad covered with glitter—but he also didn't look like a horse that was competing in a show.

"I'll try to brush it off," Ashleigh said. "Maybe that will work, but I doubt it." Ranger's box of brushes was right by the stall door, she saw, not in the tack room the way it usually was. Then she saw why—the box was empty.

Ashleigh rubbed her forehead. She tried not to panic, but it wasn't easy. *I just have to be ready in time for the show. If this is Diana's idea of the Christmas spirit, it's not very funny,* she thought as she hurried to the tack room to borrow Neptune's brushes again.

While she was trying to decide whether a dandy brush or a body brush would more effectively deal with the glitter, Ashleigh happened to glance up at the racks of saddles.

"Oh, no!" she cried. "Where is it?" Ranger's saddle had disappeared from its post.

Ashleigh stomped out of the tack room. Up the aisle, she spotted Diana flying around a corner with the saddle. "Hey!" Ashleigh yelled, running after her.

Within a few strides Ashleigh had almost caught up. She was wearing paddock sneakers, and Diana was trying to run in high black boots. Those boots, Ashleigh knew, were designed to kick a rider's weight back onto her heels, not for sprinting. Diana was also awkwardly dragging the saddle.

In front of Silverado's stall Ashleigh caught up with her and triumphantly reached to grab the saddle just as Diana was about to pitch it over the half-door.

"Diana, what are you doing with Ranger's tack?" Jane asked calmly, walking up to them.

"Helping Ashleigh clean it," Diana said immediately. "She asked my advice because she always puts too much oil on it."

Jane lifted her brows and looked at Ashleigh.

Ashleigh noticed that Diana looked scared. *I couldn't prove she did any of the other stuff to me, but this time she got caught red-handed*, Ashleigh thought. *Jane may kick her out of the show if I tell her what happened. I guess that would be pretty awful.*

"We were looking for the oil, but it isn't here," Ashleigh said. "Carry the saddle back to Ranger's stall, Diana. Maybe we should look again there."

A faint smile crossed Diana's face. "Oh, okay," she said.

"You pull dumb tricks," Ashleigh said as they walked back to the stall.

"The glitter wasn't dumb." Diana grinned.

"I hope you've got some really good ideas about how to get it off," Ashleigh said. "Because you're going to help me, for as long as it takes."

"I have to get Silverado ready!" Diana protested.

"If you desert me, I'll tell Jane exactly what's been going on since Caro and I started lessons."

Diana looked scared again. "I have to compete in the show. My dad will be furious if I don't."

"So don't complain about helping me," Ashleigh said.

Caroline was standing in front of Ranger's stall. She looked at Ashleigh in horror, then back at Ranger. "What happened to him?"

"He got glittered." Ashleigh took Ranger's saddle from Diana and balanced it on the half-door of his stall. *At least Diana didn't mess up the saddle again. I'm making progress,* Ashleigh thought.

"She did this, right?" Caroline asked, glaring at Diana.

"Yeah." Ashleigh led Ranger out of his stall, put him in crossties, and looked him over. She couldn't think about Diana now. She had to think about how to get Ranger ready for the show ring. There was no way she was going to miss the show, after all the lessons and work. She and Ranger were ready to perform.

"This is just making it go deeper into his coat," Diana complained, tossing down a body brush.

"Never mind. I'll do it," Ashleigh said absently.

"Bye," Diana said. "See you behind me when we get our ribbons."

Ashleigh didn't bother to answer.

"Aren't you mad?" Caroline asked.

"Not yet." Ashleigh frowned. "I will be if I can't get this off and be in the show."

"We should tell Jane," Caroline said.

"Maybe it's not so bad." Ashleigh studied Ranger. She decided that the stiff dandy brush would remove the glitter best and got to work.

"Do you need help?" Caroline asked. "I have to get Neptune ready, but Mom and Dad and Mona will be here in a little while. I could tell them to come over here."

"That's okay." But Ashleigh winced as she looked at her work so far. The glitter didn't seem to be coming off. It was only spreading over Ranger's coat—and to Ashleigh's clothes and hair. Ashleigh redoubled her efforts. Finally she made some progress with a soft cloth.

"Time for the English pleasure class," Jane said as Ashleigh walked out of the stable bathroom. She'd washed her hands and face and changed her clothes. She knew she still sparkled close up, but not, she hoped, from a distance.

Ranger was waiting for her in the crossties. He nickered and bobbed his head. Ashleigh checked his girth a last time. No problem there.

"Okay, boy," Ashleigh said, patting the big horse's neck. "Show time. We've worked hard. I know we can win, no matter who tries to get in our way."

Ranger bent his head and gently nudged her hands. Then he was still, as if he were thinking things over. Finally he lifted his head and tugged on the crossties.

"I'm ready, too," Ashleigh said. "Let's show everybody just how good we are."

Ashleigh mounted Ranger at the entrance to the cool, echoing ring. He still glittered a little, especially his mane and tail. Ashleigh wondered if the American Horse Shows Association rule book said somewhere that horses couldn't glitter in a show. Probably not—only Diana's mind could have thought of it.

Ashleigh walked Ranger around the ring, composing herself. The class wasn't being judged yet, but the judges had taken their seats in a booth near the ring. They were already watching. Ashleigh reminded herself to make every move of hers and Ranger's in front of the judges as perfect as possible.

She saw her parents, Rory, and Mona sitting in the bleachers. A lot of people were watching—parents, friends, and the younger riders at Chesterton, who had already ridden in their classes.

Caroline was walking Neptune on the far side of the ring. Ashleigh noticed that her sister's hands looked a little high. Diana, Barbara, and Cheryl were coming up behind Ashleigh on their horses.

I wonder if Diana and her friends will try some tricks on me in the ring, Ashleigh thought. She decided not to worry about it. The judges were experienced enough to know what was going on if something like that happened. Diana would only ruin her own chances.

Ashleigh looked between Ranger's ears. Now she felt completely relaxed and could focus on the details of her appearance—the position of her fingers, the exact angle of her calves on Ranger's sides. In the five weeks of lessons that she'd had, Ashleigh knew she and Ranger had adapted well to each other. Perfect form came naturally.

Ranger seemed to understand that they were in competition. He extended his walk without being asked and arched his neck beautifully, collecting himself. Ashleigh lost herself in the familiar rocking motion of the horse. "That's a boy," she murmured. "Show off your best."

"You are now being judged," called the announcer.

This is it! Ashleigh smiled with excitement. The show might be just a little one, but she wanted to win it. As she and Ranger walked by the judges' booth, she saw one of the judges smile back.

Ashleigh was entered in both English pleasure, in which the horse was judged, and English equitation, in which the rider was judged. She had never seen much difference between the two classes. She might not be judged in the pleasure class, but if her form was sloppy, Ranger's responses and movements would be sloppy as well. In this class Ranger was under scrutiny.

"Trot, please!" called the announcer. "Posting trot."

Ashleigh took a deep breath to compose herself and asked Ranger for a trot. They had plenty of room—all the other horses in the class were bunched at the far side of the arena.

"Halt!"

Ashleigh quickly checked Ranger, so that he stopped only a pace or two after the command was given. Jane had warned her to be very careful about doing exactly what the judges asked. "If they say stop, they don't mean walk halfway around the ring and then stop," she'd said. "Same goes for every command."

Diana had checked Silverado too hard, Ashleigh saw. The gray had stopped immediately, but he flung up his head as if his mouth hurt.

Ashleigh winced. Probably Diana hadn't really hurt Silverado that much, but the effect wasn't good.

"Circle and walk. Sitting trot," said the announcer.

Ashleigh selected Ranger's pace carefully. She wanted him to trot fast enough so that he didn't look as though he was sleeping, but slow enough so that she didn't bounce too much. Ashleigh knew she sat to the trot better than most of the other riders. She'd had years of practice riding Moe bareback.

Caroline was coming up on the outside on Neptune. He was going too fast and bouncing her a lot. She was barely managing to hang on to the reins.

Caro must be nervous, Ashleigh thought. *She doesn't usually do that badly.*

Suddenly Neptune began to drift in front of Ranger. He was going to cut Ranger off!

Get him in hand, Caroline! Ashleigh thought frantically. She couldn't talk in the class and tell her sister what to do. But in just a second Ashleigh would be forced to check Ranger sharply to avoid hitting Neptune. That would break his gait and make him look terrible.

I should have seen Neptune and Caroline coming. Ashleigh knew that she was supposed to account for the movements of other horses and avoid these problems, even if Caroline's horse had come out of nowhere and was practically running away with her.

In the next seconds Ashleigh could see that Caroline wasn't going to regain control. Ashleigh would have to check Ranger with her seat to avoid hauling on the reins.

Gradually she leaned back in the saddle. She prayed Ranger would respond to such an indirect signal. They'd practiced together for such a short time!

Ranger slowed just enough, and Neptune shot in front

of them. Ashleigh didn't let her expression show her relief. Maybe the judges would think she'd planned the whole thing perfectly.

"Canter!" said the announcer.

Ashleigh quickly put Ranger on the correct lead. This time she kept a close watch on the positions of the other horses.

The judges asked for a canter on the other lead, then lined the riders up in the center of the ring. The judges came out of their booth and paced up and down in front of the line of riders, inspecting them. Then they gathered and made notes on their clipboards.

Ashleigh swallowed nervously. She thought she'd ridden the best in the class. But there was no way of knowing how the judges would evaluate her near miss with Caroline. And Diana was wearing about a thousand dollars' worth of riding clothes. She made a great impression, Ashleigh had to admit. That might count heavily in Diana's favor.

The judges broke apart and looked around. The announcer walked over to them. "In first place, number three—Ashleigh Griffen!" he called.

Ashleigh's face broke into a huge grin. She heard a whoop from the bleachers whcre her family and Mona were sitting.

"Way to go, Ashleigh!" her dad called. Ashleigh waved at them and rode Ranger over to collect her ribbon.

"Congratulations." The judge smiled as she handed Ashleigh the blue. "You rode well—and that bit of glitter is lovely. It gives a very nice holiday effect."

"Thanks." Ashleigh almost laughed. She looked around to see if Diana had heard.

She and Silverado were right behind them to collect the second-place ribbon. Diana made a face. She'd definitely heard.

"Hey, Ashleigh, ride a victory lap!" Mona yelled.

Ashleigh wished she could. In bigger shows that was customary. But at such a small show it would probably look like grandstanding.

"Good job, Ash," Caroline said. But she looked disappointed—she'd placed last.

"Thanks." Ashleigh felt sorry for Caro.

Ashleigh's next class, English equitation, immediately followed English pleasure. Ashleigh barely had time to accept her family's congratulations before she had to remount and ride into the ring again.

"Walk, please," the announcer said.

Pay more attention to what the other horses are doing this time, Ashleigh told herself. *You just got lucky in the last class.*

Ashleigh saw Diana walking Silverado behind her. She wasn't too close—yet. Ashleigh asked Ranger for a slightly faster walk to put more distance between them.

"Posting trot," the announcer requested.

Ranger easily moved into the faster gait. He seemed to float, his hooves barely touching the ground. Ashleigh posted to the trot, instantly picking up the right diagonal so that she rose in the stirrups when Ranger's left leg was extended. Her movements felt light and supple.

I'm going to walk away with another blue ribbon! she

thought. *Let's go a little faster, so the judges see how spirited Ranger is.* Imperceptibly she shifted her weight forward in the saddle, signaling Ranger to extend his trot.

A moment later Ashleigh realized she'd been overconfident. Diana was still behind her, and she had signaled Silverado to go faster also. The beautifully trained warmblood moved out gracefully—until he and Diana were completely blocking Ashleigh and Ranger from the judges' view.

Ashleigh tried to check Ranger slightly, but he wasn't nearly as sensitive to her commands as Silverado was to Diana's. Diana had no trouble staying squarely in front of them.

If the judges can't see me, I'm not going to win anything! Ashleigh thought desperately.

"Number four, please come to the side of the ring," the announcer boomed.

Startled, Ashleigh saw Diana and Silverado veer off from beside them and trot to the side of the ring. One of the judges came out from the booth and spoke to Diana.

Ashleigh wondered briefly what he was saying, but the two other judges were sitting in the booth, still evaluating the class. *Now that Diana's gone, I bet I can really shine,* she thought with relief.

Ashleigh put Ranger through the required walk, trot, and canter of the class. She knew she looked good. She found herself almost wishing the competition were stiffer. Diana had returned to the class, but she was slouched over and not trying very hard.

The judges lined the horses up in the center of the ring again. This time they hardly conferred.

"And the blue goes to number three again, Ashleigh Griffen!" the announcer said.

Ashleigh rode over to collect her second blue ribbon. The judge fastened it to Ranger's bridle.

"Good boy!" Ashleigh praised, patting his neck. "I knew you could do it!" She was glad to see that Caroline got second in the class.

Mona and Ashleigh's parents walked into the ring, clapping.

"Way to go, Ashleigh!" Mona grinned. "Did you hear what the judge said to Diana?"

"No, what?"

"He was yelling at her for blocking you. He said that's an old, cheap trick in show classes and he wasn't going to stand for it."

"I heard part of what he was saying, too," Mrs. Griffen said. "The judge reprimanded Diana. He told her that he'd ridden in too many classes himself where the competitors pulled dirty tricks. He said he wanted Diana to learn polite show habits now, while she's young. He didn't disqualify her, but he did put her in last place."

"Wow," Ashleigh said. "That's kind of tough. I was really glad he made her move away from us, though."

Ranger stamped his foot impatiently. "I know, I promised you carrots if you did a good job," Ashleigh told him. "You couldn't have been more wonderful in the show. You did everything I asked and looked perfectly beautiful. And you didn't try to bite Silverado when he got so close to us, even though you had every right to."

"I guess that's the last time Diana will call him a stable nag," Caroline said.

"You bet," Ashleigh said with satisfaction.

Ashleigh untacked the gelding and put him in his stall. Then she looked around. She half expected a bucket of water to fall on her head. "I'm so sick of Diana's tricks," she murmured. "At least over the Christmas break I'll have Ranger to ride and I won't have to see Diana and her friends. I could use a rest from chasing saddles and brushes and cleaning weird things off my horse!"

Ranger shook his head, as if he disapproved of the whole thing, too. Ashleigh looked at the traces of glitter on him and laughed. "I'll see you soon, boy. You're going to have a great time with Neptune and Caro and me. We'll go for a ride every day!"

Caroline was putting Neptune's brushes in his bucket when Ashleigh walked by the stall. "Ready?" Caroline asked. Ashleigh nodded.

Outside, the early winter night was falling. The last orange of the sunset rimmed gray clouds in the sky. A cold breeze lifted the girls' hair. Ashleigh looked for the Griffens' truck, but she didn't see it yet.

"I can't wait for Ranger and Neptune to be at Edgardale," Ashleigh said. "We'll get them in just two weeks, after Jane's last riding class before the holidays. Then for two weeks after that we'll have our very own riding horses. Won't that be super?"

"Yeah," Caroline said. "I really want to get away from Jane."

"You don't want to quit the lessons, do you?" Ashleigh asked. Caro didn't seem to like them much.

"No. I think Mom and Dad would be really disappointed if I did." Caroline sighed. "You're lucky, Ashleigh. You're interested in horses the way Mom and Dad are. I like horses and everything, but . . ."

"But you don't want to own a breeding farm when you grow up," Ashleigh finished.

"Right. Mom and Dad don't get that sometimes." Caroline frowned. "Isn't that Diana standing over there? What's she doing?"

Ashleigh looked over where Caroline was pointing. Diana was standing at the end of the drive, hanging her head. *I bet she feels bad about losing in the show today,* Ashleigh thought. "I guess she's waiting for her ride," she said.

"She acts like nobody's coming. Maybe we should ask if she wants to come with us," Caroline said. "She looks so lonesome."

At that moment a silver Porsche roared up the drive. The Griffens' pickup followed.

"That's her dad's car," Ashleigh said. *Good,* she thought. Ashleigh felt sorry for Diana, but that didn't mean she wanted to ride all the way home with her.

9

Ashleigh awoke to a strange, muted light coming through the window. She hurried to the window and gasped with pleasure. Snow in Kentucky on Christmas Day! That almost never happened. The rolling hills were soft white humps, broken only by the half-covered fence posts. The thickly coated barn looked like a white gingerbread house.

"Ash! Caro!" Rory bounded into the room and grabbed Ashleigh's hand. "We have to open presents!"

"Yeah!" Ashleigh said excitedly. "Come on, Caroline."

Slowly Caroline's face appeared over the edge of her comforter. "It's too early," she mumbled.

"The sun's almost up. It's practically seven." Ashleigh yanked the comforter off her sister. "Mom and Dad must have fed the horses for us."

"Hurry, Caro!" Rory urged.

"Oh, all right. I'm not going to get another minute of

93

sleep with you two around." Caroline sat up and stretched. "Merry Christmas!"

"Merry Christmas!" Rory yelled. Ashleigh pounded down the stairs with Rory at her heels.

In the living room their parents had already turned the tree lights on. The day outside was overcast, and the soft blue, red, and green of the lights made the room especially warm and inviting. Colorful packages were stacked under the tree, and striped stockings hung from the mantelpiece, weighted down with small presents and candy. From the kitchen came the fragrant smell of pancakes cooking.

Rory rushed at his pile of presents.

"Slow down!" said Mrs. Griffen, laughing. "Wait for Caroline."

"I'm here," Caroline called from the stairs.

"All right!" Rory yelled.

Ashleigh tore into her presents almost as eagerly as Rory. She got three new horse books—one about training, one about dressage, and one a novel about a famous Thoroughbred filly racehorse. Ashleigh pictured herself curled up in bed at night, cozy in her comforter as she devoured the books.

"I can't wait to read them! Thanks!" she told her parents.

Caroline had gotten two new sweaters and a matching wool scarf and hat. Ashleigh knew how disappointed she would be if she got only clothes for Christmas, but Caroline looked thrilled.

Rory was already lining up a new set of little metal soldiers. "We can play with these guys while we're home from school, Ash, can't we?" he pleaded.

"Sure," Ashleigh said. Rory was always looking for someone to play with. The Griffens had very few neighbors, and none of them had children Rory's age.

"I want to ride Moe, too, while we don't have school," Rory said. "Ash, would you teach me some more?"

"As soon as the snow melts and it isn't so slippery," Ashleigh promised. "Probably by tomorrow."

"That should be possible," Mrs. Griffen agreed. "Snow doesn't usually stick around long here."

"Then we'd better build a snowman today," Rory said.

Ashleigh smiled at him. There was so much to do when they didn't have school! Christmas break stretched before her as deliciously as the snow. "I want to wish the horses a merry Christmas first," she said. "Then we'll build *three* snowmen, Rory—a mother, a father, and a baby snowman."

Ashleigh ate breakfast quickly, then dressed warmly in a parka and gloves. She pushed open the door and smiled in delight. The farm was a white, glorious wonderland. The previous night's storm had cleared off, and the sky was a deep blue. The snow sparkled like gems in the bright sun. Ashleigh plowed through the thick, cold snow. It was still perfectly smooth, except for the tiny tracks of birds dotting the surface and her parents' steps to and from the barn.

In the barn most of the horses were impatiently looking out over their stall doors. Because of the snow, they had to stay inside. Ashleigh knew that her parents were afraid the horses would slip and fall, especially the mares. All of them except Gallantry were very pregnant and moved awkwardly. Some were due to foal in less than a month.

"You're hoping for some excitement, aren't you?" Ashleigh asked. At least the barn looked festive, since the horses had to look at it all day. She had decorated each horse's stall with a small wreath made of pine branches, placed carefully to the side of each door so that they couldn't reach around and eat it.

Ashleigh went down to Ranger's stall to check on him. He seemed to have settled in easily since the day before, when Jane had brought him over in the school's two-horse trailer. The chestnut whickered affectionately and leaned toward her over his stall door.

Ashleigh heard hammering from the center of the barn. She didn't need to look around to know who that was. "Gallantry, quit it!" she called, walking up to the bay mare's stall.

Gallantry glanced at her for a moment. Then she kicked the stall hard. The boards shivered. "I know. Even the paddock isn't big enough for you, and this is worse." Ashleigh sighed. She didn't like to see the mare so unhappy. Ashleigh's parents didn't know what to do, either. Somebody had come out to look at Gallantry the other day, and Ashleigh assumed her parents had called in another trainer to ask for advice about how to handle her.

Ashleigh stepped across the aisle to the feed room and picked up a half-full bag of sweet feed. "I've got a treat for you," she said to Gallantry, holding out a handful of the sticky, molasses-rich feed. All the horses loved it.

Gallantry quickly lipped up the treat and craned her neck, looking for more.

"Okay," Ashleigh said. "I guess another Christmas

present won't hurt. You probably need cheering up the most."

Gallantry seemed to appreciate the second handful of feed. To Ashleigh's relief, she stopped kicking the stall. *Dad said if he has to fix that stall one more time, he'll sell her*, Ashleigh thought. *I guess he just means if she isn't happy here, she should be sold*. Ashleigh hated to think of the beautiful mare leaving the farm.

She walked down the aisle, pulling the bag of sweet feed behind her and giving each horse a handful. "Merry Christmas," she said to each one.

Caroline walked into the barn. "You're crazy, you know that?" she said. She was wearing her new scarf and hat.

"Why? Don't you think the horses should have a merry Christmas, too?" Ashleigh countered.

"I guess I can't argue with that." Caroline grinned and reached into the bag of feed. "Here, I'll help you. Then let's go build our snow people with Rory. He's about to burst."

"Come on, Ash!" Rory urged, trotting Moe ahead of Ranger.

Ashleigh asked Ranger for an extended walk and passed the little pony again. She was glad they could get out for a ride that afternoon. The snow had melted from the lanes around the farm. Drips from the eaves of the house and barn plopped onto the wet snow.

Caroline followed on Neptune. She looked much more relaxed now that they were away from Chesterton. "Where should we go?" she asked.

"Just around on the lanes where the snow has melted." Ashleigh turned left to go by the big back paddock. "Horses can't handle snow very well," she added. "It balls up in their hooves, and they could wrench an ankle."

"I know, Ashleigh," Caroline said. She sounded a little irritated. "I live in the same place you do, remember?"

"Oh, right." Ashleigh knew she sounded like a know-it-all about horses sometimes.

They rode alongside the fence surrounding the back paddock. In the summer, the paddock was covered with thick grass and sprinkled with flowers. Now it was a vast expanse of white, unbroken snow.

Ashleigh pulled up Ranger, and Caroline and Rory stopped, too. The silence was as perfect as the snow. Then, in the distance, a lone bird trilled.

"It's so beautiful out here," Caroline murmured.

A gust of wind swirled the snow in a cold shower around them and blew off Caroline's hat. Laughing, Caroline dismounted and forged through the deep snow in the paddock to retrieve it.

Ashleigh and Rory got off their horses, too. Ashleigh ran a hand through a drift, enjoying the cold on her hand. Ranger stood behind her, hanging his head and looking dubious. Ranger was a stable horse, and Ashleigh wasn't too sure how he felt about the great outdoors when it looked like this.

But Moe was energetically plunging his nose into the snow. "Moe's eating it," Rory said with a laugh.

"Can you believe we had picnics here just a couple of months ago?" Ashleigh asked.

"I guess," Rory said. "But it would be awfully cold to sit down now."

"Or if somebody threw a snowball at you—like this!" Caroline whipped a big snowball into Ashleigh's back.

"This means war!" Rory yelled, looping Moe's reins over his arm so that he could gather up snow.

They pelted each other with huge, damp snowballs.

"I give up," Caroline gasped after a while. "Look at Neptune!"

Ashleigh grinned. Caro had hidden behind Neptune during the battle, and the gray horse had big spots of snow on his side and hindquarters. He looked like an Appaloosa.

After the snowball battle they all lay down and made angels.

"Mine's the best," Rory said proudly.

"Almost good enough to fly to heaven." Ashleigh glanced up.

The fiercely colored banners of the winter sunset stretched across the sky. The sun had already dipped below the horizon. Ashleigh frowned. She hadn't meant to stay out so late. It would be hard to see the footing on the way home.

"Let's head back," she said. "The melted snow will have started to freeze into ice again on the lanes."

"We should help with feeding and dinner anyway," Caroline said as they got back on their horses.

"Rory, watch out—some of the dark patches that were water this afternoon are probably ice now," Ashleigh said.

"Okay," Rory answered. Ashleigh wasn't too worried about him and Moe. The surefooted little Shetland could handle almost any kind of terrain. She wasn't sure about Ranger and Neptune, though.

Ashleigh led them back, slowly picking a path around anything that looked dark and icy. *Almost home,* she thought when they reached the gravel driveway. *Good—I can barely see.*

An old truck was crawling up the driveway, carefully navigating the slippery patches. *That must be Dr. Thurman, coming out to check the mares in foal,* Ashleigh thought.

Suddenly a sharp report as loud as a gunshot ripped through the air. Ashleigh realized Dr. Thurman's old truck had backfired. With a squeal of terror Neptune reared, almost unseating Caroline. The next second he charged back down the lane at a dead run.

"Pull him up, Caroline!" Ashleigh screamed. "He'll slip!"

"I can't!" Caroline screamed back. Her voice was filled with terror.

"Rory, get off Moe and hang on to him tight. Find Dr. Thurman or Mom and Dad while I go after them!" Ashleigh ordered.

Rory immediately dismounted and grabbed Moe's reins. Not wasting another second, Ashleigh urged Ranger into a full gallop. She knew they were going dangerously fast—Ranger might slip, too. But as long as he didn't go down, Ashleigh knew she could keep her seat.

Ashleigh was terrified for her sister, but she kept her wits about her. Usually it didn't help to chase a runaway horse with another horse. The pursuit just made the runaway go faster. But Neptune was already running flat out. And Caroline was about to fall. Even in the dim light Ashleigh could see Caroline almost fall to one side.

"Help!" Caroline screamed.

If only she would pick a snowdrift and jump off into it! Ashleigh thought, gritting her teeth. But Caroline must be frozen with fear. Now it was up to Neptune to decide where they went.

A large white hump loomed ahead of Ashleigh. There was no time to go around it. Ashleigh remembered that Jane had said she used Ranger in jumping classes. Stadium jumping or cross-country? Ashleigh was about to find out.

Ranger soared over the obstacle with feet to spare, but on the landing he slipped and fell to his knees. Ashleigh hauled back on the reins, trying to help him regain his balance. Ranger staggered upright and charged on. Ashleigh didn't dare think what he might have done to his knees.

"Good boy!" she gasped. Ranger was showing so much heart!

Ahead of them Neptune was slipping and sliding. His reins flapped in the wind as he galloped toward the woods.

The woods, with their low-hanging branches and obstacles everywhere, would be even more dangerous than the lane. Ashleigh knew she had to put a stop to this mad dash before one of the horses fell and killed somebody. She urged Ranger to go faster.

Ranger began to draw even with Neptune. His Thoroughbred blood was showing. *We're going to win this race,* Ashleigh realized with relief. "Hang on a little longer, Caro!" she shouted. Ashleigh leaned over in her saddle to grab Neptune's reins.

Then Ashleigh saw the black, glistening surface of the ice under the horses' feet. The next second Neptune slipped on the patch and went down. He hit the ice on his side with a sickening thud.

Caroline screamed. The next moment she pitched headfirst into the snow.

Ashleigh glanced ahead. Ranger was slipping—and he was headed straight for a tree! Ashleigh summoned every bit of strength she had and hauled his head around with the reins. Even if that threw him so far off balance that he fell, it was better than hitting a tree at thirty miles an hour.

Ranger lurched and slid sideways. For several seconds Ashleigh thought he was going to go down, too. Desperately she clutched his mane, gripping with her knees. Miraculously Ranger found his footing and stayed upright. "That's the way," Ashleigh said, trying to catch her breath. "Good boy!" She jumped off and led him across the ice to where Caroline had fallen. "Caro? *Caroline!*"

Caroline lay very still. She had lost her hat again, and her new scarf half covered her face.

"Caroline? Please talk to me," Ashleigh begged. Her heart was thumping crazily with fear.

Caroline didn't move or speak. Ashleigh pulled the scarf away from her sister's head. Her hand came away covered with warm, sticky blood.

10

"COMING THROUGH!" THE AMBULANCE ATTENDANT YELLED at the Griffens. He and another attendant pulled Caroline's gurney through the emergency room entrance at the hospital.

Stunned, Ashleigh flattened herself against the wall. A final set of doors that read NO ADMITTANCE slammed behind her parents as they rushed after the gurney.

Rory was crying. "Let's go sit over here," Ashleigh said. She took her little brother's hand and led him to a row of plastic chairs. Ashleigh pulled him close.

"Is Caro going to be okay?" he whispered.

"Sure. You were wonderful to run and get Dr. Thurman so fast when Caroline got hurt. He helped her, and now the doctors can." Ashleigh prayed that was true.

After a few sniffles, Rory fell asleep with his head in her lap. *How can Christmas end like this?* Ashleigh wondered miserably. They'd all been so happy just a couple of hours earlier.

Mrs. Griffen had called Jane at home and asked her to come take care of Ranger and Neptune. Neptune seemed to be just bruised from his fall. But shreds of skin hung from Ranger's knees, and they were bleeding badly. Jane was going to call the vet and move the horses back to Chesterton that night if possible.

That was the end of Ashleigh's having her own horse. But it didn't seem to matter, when no one knew if Caroline would even live.

Finally Ashleigh's head drooped on top of Rory's. *I'll just sleep for a minute,* she thought. *I don't want to miss anything.*

"Ashleigh?" Her dad was shaking her.

Ashleigh jerked awake. She'd been dreaming that she was riding Ranger after Caroline again, but that they were in a real race at the track. Caroline was screaming. Ranger pounded up to Neptune, and this time Ashleigh could reach his reins. But the image of Caroline faded, and Ranger powered into the lead. An announcer was calling the race at Churchill Downs.

How could Ranger be in a race? He was only part Thoroughbred. She must be riding some other horse. Ashleigh shook her head. "How's Caro?" she asked quickly.

Mr. Griffen looked exhausted. "She's got a skull fracture and several superficial head injuries. She's stabilized but still unconscious. Your mom's going to stay with her while I take you and Rory home. It's four o'clock in the morning—we've got to feed the horses soon."

"Can I see her?" Ashleigh asked. Her dad looked more than exhausted, she realized. He looked scared, too.

"Sweetie, that's not possible tonight," Mr. Griffen said gently. "Caroline's still in intensive care. . . ." Mr. Griffen's voice broke. "No children are allowed in there. You can see her when she's well enough to be in a regular room." He picked up Rory, who didn't wake.

Ashleigh slowly followed her father through the door to the parking lot. *I've never been away from Caroline during my whole life, and now I can't even see her,* she thought, fighting down panic. *It's going to be really lonesome in our room when I get home.*

"I heard about Caroline," Diana said.

Ashleigh kept walking toward her bus through the crowds of kids. It was only the first day back at school after the Christmas vacation, but Ashleigh was so tired that if she stopped moving, she didn't think she could get going again.

Caroline had been in a coma for nearly two weeks. Ashleigh had been taking care of Rory and doing most of the chores around the farm while her parents spent every possible minute at the hospital. That morning she'd fed all the horses and put them out in the paddocks, then she'd mucked out eighteen stalls. After school she'd have to phone the feed store owner and talk to him about substituting another kind of feed for the one her parents had ordered, which was out of stock. Then she'd have to schedule the vet's visit and discuss with the horseshoer how to correct a hoof problem one of the mares had.

Every day she had to do as much or more. Ashleigh just wondered how long she could keep it up.

If Diana says one word about how bad a rider Caroline is, I'm going to hit her, Ashleigh thought.

"I'm sorry about what happened," Diana went on. "That's tough."

Ashleigh turned in surprise. Diana, Barbara, and Cheryl all stood there. For once, nobody was sneering.

"Thanks," she said.

"Ranger's doing okay," Diana added.

"Yeah, I know. Jane called. He just has cuts—nothing major." Ashleigh had almost cried with relief when she'd heard Ranger had come through their wild ride all right. He'd been so heroic the night Caroline fell. He hadn't refused a single command Ashleigh had given him, even though she'd put him in danger and through a lot of pain. "Ranger's a great horse," Ashleigh added.

"That's true." Diana nodded. "Jane told us what he did."

I never thought I'd hear Diana say that. Ashleigh started walking toward her bus again.

"Are you quitting lessons?" Diana caught up to her.

"I don't know." Ashleigh shrugged. She hadn't really thought about it. She just had to get through each day.

Diana grinned. "Well, if you do come back, I might give you and Ranger a break for a while. Just until Caroline's better."

Ashleigh smiled a little. "I'll think about it. I'm pretty busy at home."

"Ashleigh! Come on!" Mona was calling from the steps of the bus.

"See you," Ashleigh said. Diana waved.

"What did she want?" Mona asked as Ashleigh sat down next to her on the bus.

"To say she was sorry about Caro."

"Really?" Mona looked surprised. "Diana's so selfish, I'm surprised she cared at all."

"Maybe she isn't so bad. Nothing she did ever really hurt anyone." Ashleigh pressed her forehead against the window glass. The Christmas snow had completely melted, and the asphalt schoolyard was covered with foot-long puddles that reflected the gray sky. Edgardale was a muddy mess. "And Diana never did anything mean to Caroline," Ashleigh added.

"Someone wants to see you!" Mrs. Griffen said, poking her head around the doorway to Ashleigh's room the next day after school.

"Caroline?" Ashleigh cried, jumping up from her desk. "She's awake?"

"She's awake and talking," Mrs. Griffen said. Ashleigh had never seen her mother look so happy. "Come on. She's asking for you."

"I'll stay with Rory," Mr. Griffen called from the living room. "One person's enough company for Caroline right now."

Ashleigh raced for the truck. She'd never had a better reason to quit doing her homework. She could hardly believe that the nightmare of the last two weeks was over.

At the hospital Mrs. Griffen led the way down a wide,

antiseptic-smelling hall to Caroline's room and opened the door.

"Caro?" Ashleigh whispered.

Caroline lay on a big bed with her eyes closed. Ashleigh tiptoed over to her and sank into a hard plastic chair next to the bed.

Caroline's eyes flew open. "Ashleigh! Hi!"

"How are you feeling?" Ashleigh asked. Then she wondered if she should have asked. Tubes ran into both of Caroline's arms, and the skin around her eyes was black and sunken. Ashleigh didn't see how her sister could feel anything but terrible.

"Not too bad." Caroline winced as she moved one of her arms. "I can't believe I was unconscious for two weeks. And I don't remember anything about the fall."

That's good, Ashleigh thought. *I wish I didn't.*

"So how are the lessons going?" Caroline asked.

"Well . . . I missed one today. I haven't really been riding."

"Because of me. You have to do all the chores." Caroline sighed.

"I don't mind," Ashleigh said. It was so good to see her sister awake and talking again. Anything was worth that. "I really don't care about missing the lessons," she added.

Caroline shifted in the bed. "Ashleigh, you just have to go back and ride. I didn't tell you this because I thought you'd get a big head, but I heard Jane say to another instructor that you're the best rider she's seen in ten years of teaching. Look, you don't have to be here. I'm coming home tomorrow, and I'm going to be fine."

"Thanks for telling me about Jane." Ashleigh yawned. But even though she was exhausted, she felt a flicker of excitement at Caroline's words. Her life had been so empty without riding. She remembered the supple feel of the leather reins in her hands, the sudden burst of speed and the slap of the wind in her face as Moe switched to a gallop.

"I'll definitely go back to riding now that you're better." Ashleigh smiled at her sister. "Don't worry—I wouldn't ever give it up."

"Okay, Sunstorm. This is your dress rehearsal for the auction." Ashleigh rubbed her hands. The winter afternoon was barely heated by the pallid, sinking sun, but she didn't like to wear gloves when she worked the horses. Gloved hands weren't nearly as sensitive as bare ones.

She led the gray colt into the stable yard and stopped him. "Just two more days. Then you've got to impress a ringful of people."

The big colt pricked up his ears at her words. He looked relaxed but alert, just the way he should.

Ashleigh's heart ached with pride as she looked at him. The colt was absolutely gorgeous. As he grew older, his coat had lightened in patches of gray that looked like the spotty silver of a cloudy sky. His slender, graceful legs, no longer the gangly stilts of a foal, smoothly angled into his muscular, well-proportioned shoulders and body.

The big colt lovingly pushed her hands with his nose. "Sweetie," Ashleigh said, scratching him behind the ears.

"I wish I could put in the auction program everything you like, so that your new owner will know just what to do." *If he wants to,* she thought with a chill. She knew that some owners bought racehorses only to make money.

Mr. Griffen walked up, leading Southern Sky. The bay filly balked, digging in her heels and pulling against the lead rope. "Come on, girl," Mr. Griffen coaxed. Sky tossed her small, elegant head and at last decided to follow him. Mr. Griffen was getting the filly ready for the auction as well.

Ashleigh looked at her father. "I wish they didn't have to go," she said. "Especially Sunstorm."

"I know." Mr. Griffen patted Ashleigh's shoulder. "But we have to do what makes business sense. Your mom and I plan to use the money from Sunstorm's sale to buy a mare named Slewette, the daughter of a Triple Crown champion. She's already in foal."

"Mom told me. I think Sun's almost ready." Ashleigh knew that her parents' business had to run the way it did. She couldn't sulk because the horses had to be sold.

Sunstorm switched his silky tail. Ashleigh smoothed aside his forelock. Sunstorm had a thick, long mane and tail, like an Arabian. It added greatly to his beauty.

"He looks fine." Mr. Griffen studied the colt. "Couldn't be better. He's going to turn a lot of heads at Keeneland."

Ashleigh swallowed. "I think so, too. But Dad . . . what if his new owners aren't nice to him? Remember that story you told me about those people who pushed their horse too fast as a two-year-old and ruined his legs?"

"Well . . ." Her dad hesitated. "It's true, that happens. But not usually with a horse of this caliber. Those people I told you about medicated the horse so that he wouldn't feel the pain in his legs. Then they ran him, thinking they'd get one more race out of him. They didn't—he broke down in the race and had to be destroyed. It's not in an owner's interest to mistreat a horse, Ashleigh. Some people are fools and do it anyway, but I don't think we need to worry about Sunstorm."

"I hope not." Ashleigh ran a loving hand over the colt's back.

"I'm going to put Sky in the barn and phone a breeder I know about a horse. He's giving her away! Can you imagine? Call if you need me."

"Okay." Ashleigh wondered what kind of horse somebody would give away. Probably it was nineteen years old, swaybacked, and toothless.

Ashleigh looked at Sunstorm. The magnificent colt stood quietly, his neck arched. He thrust his elegant nose into the air and sniffed. Then he leaned over and tucked his head under Ashleigh's arm.

"I know, we won't need Dad to help," Ashleigh said. "Unless it's to get you out of my pocket! I think you're gentle enough. What else do we need to work on?"

Sunstorm gave her an affectionate push.

"Okay, we'll get going," Ashleigh said. "Let's play auction. Walk, boy."

The big colt kept up with her perfectly, walking on her right side. If anything, he stayed a little too close.

"Now trot." Ashleigh gave an almost imperceptible tug

on the lead line. Sunstorm instantly broke into a trot, and they circled the stable yard. Ashleigh had to run to keep up with the colt's long strides.

"Whoa!" Sunstorm skidded to a stop and looked to her for directions. "Good. Now they're going to bid on you." Ashleigh noticed that she wasn't breathing hard at all. The past two and a half months of conditioning Sunstorm had gotten her in shape, too. "Stand nice and straight. . . ." Carefully she arranged the colt's legs until he was standing perfectly square.

Ashleigh backed away from Sunstorm to study her work. A lump formed in her throat. The colt stood stock still, his finely molded head turned slightly on his crested neck. He was beautiful enough to be a statue.

Sunstorm cocked his head and looked at her. His dark eyes were questioning. He seemed to be asking, *Am I doing okay?*

Ashleigh's heart melted. She threw her arms around him.

"You did really well, boy," she assured him. But she didn't want to play the auction game anymore. Suddenly it wasn't any fun at all.

11

ASHLEIGH WALKED WITH HER PARENTS THROUGH THE manicured, spacious auction grounds at Keeneland. The morning was still chilly, and most of the dozens of horses walking with their grooms were blanketed or sheeted.

I'm not really sure I want to be here, Ashleigh thought, zipping up her parka. She didn't care about the cold. But in less than an hour Sunstorm would be auctioned. Agonizing as it would be to see the colt sold, Ashleigh felt she had to be with him on his last day as the Griffens' horse.

This sale was for horses of all ages, and so broodmares, racehorses, and yearlings walked with their grooms across the yard outside the barns. Inside, last-minute grooming preparations were under way. Ashleigh had just given Sunstorm a final brushing.

It would be the very last one she ever gave him, unless by some fluke he didn't meet his reserve. Ashleigh knew her parents had set a minimum price for Sunstorm. If it wasn't met, they would take him home again. That was her only chance to keep him. But it wouldn't be under very happy circumstances.

She'd left him moments before in the stall her parents had rented. The colt had stuck his handsome head out over the door, looking eagerly after her. He probably wondered when she was going to take him out. Ashleigh had hurried away before she broke down in tears.

"I see a lot of quality horses at this sale," Mrs. Griffen said.

"That bodes well for us," Mr. Griffen agreed.

So much for hoping Sunstorm won't meet his reserve, Ashleigh thought. She had to admit that everywhere she looked, she saw elegant, well-conditioned horses. Most of them were giving their handlers a lot more trouble than Sunstorm had ever given her. As she watched, a tall, rangy black stallion rose into the air, pawing the sky with his hooves. The next second he yanked free from his groom and rushed across the yard, scattering horses, grooms, and bystanders.

Several people cried out as the stallion ran in circles. Moving to the young stallion's side, a groom from another barn carefully reached out and grabbed his rope.

"Good, that man put a stop to that," Mrs. Griffen said with relief. "A loose stallion could easily have hurt himself or another horse."

"That incident is unfortunate for his owners. A lot of the people here are buyers," Mr. Griffen said. "When he's in the auction ring, they'll remember that he's hard to handle."

Sunstorm certainly wouldn't run away like that, Ashleigh thought glumly. *I almost wish I hadn't trained him so well—then he'd make a bad impression like that horse, and we might get to take him home again.*

Her parents entered the auction building and stood at the back of the already considerable crowd. Ashleigh thought a minute. At the back with her parents, she could hardly see the auction ring. That might be better—it would wrench her heart to be near her beloved colt but unable to touch him or talk to him. But at the front, near the ring, she would be close to him one last time. Ashleigh knew she couldn't pass up that chance.

She began to worm her way through the buyers and spectators. Finally she was right next to the rail. No one seemed to mind that she had pushed in front—she was definitely the shortest person there.

"Our first horse, ladies and gentlemen, is a bay filly out of Dare Me Now, by Revolutionary," the auctioneer announced. "Do I hear an opening bid of ten thousand for this splendid young horse?"

Ashleigh watched the bay horse walk around the ring. Her muscles stood out under her gleaming coat. She had a perfect diamond star and a beautiful, finely shaped head. *I'd pay ten thousand dollars for her,* Ashleigh decided. *That is, if I had it—I think I have just ten dollars, period.*

The first horse sold for twenty thousand dollars. The next horse went for twenty-five thousand. Ashleigh gripped the rail tensely. She didn't know whether to be proud Sunstorm was in such high-class company or unhappy because the colt would almost certainly make his reserve. As the auction went on, most of the horses sold for what seemed to her very high prices.

Sunstorm was the eleventh horse called into the ring. A handler led the colt around. Sunstorm followed the man easily, his walk light and graceful. He kept a step behind, just the way he and Ashleigh had practiced so many times.

A ripple of murmured admiration passed through the crowd as Sunstorm stopped, tossed his black-and-white mane, and looked out at them. Ashleigh swallowed hard. That was her colt—every sleek, well-conditioned inch of him. But only for another minute.

"Do I hear thirty thousand for this yearling?" the auctioneer asked.

Ashleigh looked around at her parents and saw the shock on their faces. She knew they had never expected the bidding to start so high. They would have been happy to go home with that much.

"I have thirty," the auctioneer said. "Do I hear thirty-five?"

Sunstorm threw up his head and paced nervously in a circle. He kept looking out into the crowd. The bidding went up and up, but Ashleigh barely heard. *He's looking for me,* she realized. "I can't come to you," she said. She knew he couldn't hear her over the rustling and conversation of the crowd, but maybe somehow he would get the message. "But I promise you this is for the best. You're going to race—what could be more exciting than that?"

Suddenly Sunstorm saw her. His ears pricked, and he strained against the lead line. For a moment Ashleigh thought the colt was going to run toward her. "No," she said softly. "You can't, sweetie. That's not what you're supposed to do."

Her long training paid off. Sunstorm stayed where he was, watching her.

If only I could be up there for a few seconds, Ashleigh thought. Her throat was tight. *For just a little longer. Maybe then I could think of some way to say good-bye that wouldn't hurt so much.*

"Sold!" the auctioneer called triumphantly. "Sold to the gentleman from Russet Farms!"

Ashleigh vaguely registered that Russet Farms was where Rambunctious, the previous year's Travers Stakes winner, lived. It was one of the richest training and breeding farms in Kentucky. But that didn't mean much to her now.

The handler tugged on Sunstorm's lead. The auction was over for him. Someone from the new owner's farm would be waiting outside to take him to his new home. The colt followed the handler obediently out of the ring, but his head was still twisted around as he searched for Ashleigh.

He doesn't understand that he's never going to see me again, Ashleigh thought. She squeezed her eyes shut, trying to keep back the tears. *I wish I could understand it.*

"Eighty thousand dollars!" Mr. Griffen said, beaming. "And Southern Sky brought twenty thousand!" The Griffens stood just outside the auction building at Keeneland. All around them horses were clopping by as the handlers led them to and from the auction ring. Ashleigh couldn't help looking for Sunstorm, although she wasn't sure if it would be good if she did see him.

"I just can't believe it—an Edgardale colt commanded the highest price at the sale so far!" Mrs. Griffen shook her head. "I'm dazed."

Ashleigh tried to smile. This was great news for her parents. But she didn't see Sunstorm. He was gone for good.

"I thought we'd have to sell Moon Bright and the other yearlings at the Keeneland September sale, but now I'm sure some of them will be chosen for the select sale in July," Mrs. Griffen said. "Thanks to Sunstorm."

"That's great," Ashleigh managed to say, her voice choked.

Mrs. Griffen looked at her with concern. "Dad and I can't thank you enough for what you did with Sunstorm. He couldn't have looked or handled better."

"I'm glad it was worth it." At that moment, though, Ashleigh didn't think it was worth it at all. Her parents had gotten a great price for a horse, and a lot more people had heard of Edgardale now. But Ashleigh felt terrible.

"Sunstorm's on his way to becoming the next Triple Derby," Mr. Griffen said.

"He's got the look of a horse that could go the classic distances—a good, deep chest and strong, well-proportioned legs," Mrs. Griffen added. "It will be exciting to follow his career."

Ashleigh knew her parents were trying to cheer her up, but it wasn't working.

"Let's go straight home and celebrate with everybody," Mrs. Griffen said, walking toward the parking lot. "Caroline could probably use some help with Rory by now."

"I'll bet," Ashleigh agreed. Caroline had been baby-sitting Rory while they were at the auction. Rory had insisted that he would take care of Caroline, who still didn't have all her strength back. But being around Rory wasn't usually very restful.

Ashleigh didn't feel like celebrating. Now more than ever she needed a horse of her own, a horse that wouldn't be sold after one short year. "Mom . . ." Ashleigh's voice trembled. "Since Sunstorm made so much money in the sale, can I have a horse now?"

"Ashleigh, we haven't forgotten you," her mother said quickly. "But this sounds like more money than it is. We've got a lot of mouths to feed, both horses and people. We can't quite afford a horse for you."

Ashleigh threw herself into the backseat of the truck. *I've heard that before.* She could feel tears starting in her eyes. If her parents didn't buy her a horse when they had this much money, they were never going to. They just didn't want her to have a horse.

Now I don't have Sunstorm, she thought. *Now I don't have anybody.*

Ashleigh blinked back tears. She knew her parents would think she was crying because she hadn't gotten her way about the horse, but that wasn't the main reason.

Ashleigh tried to comfort herself by imagining Sunstorm at the track. For a moment she saw the beautiful colt as he would look in a year, walking proudly in the post parade, then flying out of the starting gate to lead a thundering field in a wire-to-wire finish. The colt would love the excitement of racing.

But then she saw the colt's forlorn dark eyes as he searched the crowd for her while the handler led him away.

12

"LOOK AT THIS, ASHLEIGH!" MONA CANTERED FRISKY IN A tight circle in the stable yard at Edgardale. Then she cued her to make a flying lead change at the center of the circle and completed the figure eight. "What do you think?" she called.

"Great!" Ashleigh tried to smile. But her patience was wearing thin. Mona had already been showing off on Frisky for half an hour. Mona's timing couldn't have been worse. Ashleigh still felt bad about losing Sunstorm at the auction the day before.

Mona pulled Frisky up in front of her. "My trainer says Frisky may have some talent at dressage," she said breathlessly. "Frisky's built right, with her weight up front."

"Wow. Can I ride her?" Ashleigh asked. Mona had offered to let Ashleigh ride weeks earlier, but so far she hadn't made the slightest move to share the horse.

"Well—sure." Mona slowly dismounted.

"If you don't want me to, I don't have to," Ashleigh said angrily.

"Let's not fight about it again." Mona looked uncertain. "It's just hard to do something my trainer told me not to. I mean, he said other people riding my horse might wreck her."

"I'm not going to *wreck* your horse!" Ashleigh cried.

"Here, go ahead." Mona sighed and handed her the reins.

I really don't even want to ride now, Ashleigh thought. But if she didn't, they would probably have another fight. She swung into the saddle and adjusted the reins.

Ashleigh could tell instantly that she was on a Thoroughbred. Frisky's powerful muscles quivered, and she threw up her head. The mare danced sideways, upset by the new rider. Ashleigh pulled firmly on the reins. She had a lot of horse under her, and she needed to show Frisky right away who was boss.

"Don't jerk her mouth!" Mona cried.

"If I can't use the reins, how am I supposed to stop her?" Ashleigh asked in exasperation. Mona was her best friend, but she was really being rotten. Frisky sensed the tension in the air and lifted her front hooves off the ground, almost rearing.

Using her heels sharply, Ashleigh forced the mare to walk forward. Frisky walked a couple of steps, then crabstepped again, flicking her tail nervously. Ashleigh used her heels again. "Come on, girl. That's enough acting up." Frisky leaped forward, shaking her head. Ashleigh was forced to tighten up on the reins again.

Frisky knows I'm afraid to really make her mind, since Mona's watching, Ashleigh thought. *This isn't going to work.*

Frisky's neck was darkening with sweat. Mona was clenching and unclenching her hands.

"Forget it," Ashleigh said. She dismounted and handed the reins back to Mona. "I don't want to upset both of you."

"I'm sorry," Mona said. "But I just got her. I'm still figuring out how to handle her myself, and she's acting confused with you."

Ashleigh frowned. Maybe Mona was right. She knew that even some racehorses had a definite preference for one rider over another. They couldn't be ridden by just anybody. She took a deep breath. "It's okay. Maybe I'd feel the same way about my horse—if I had a horse."

"I'm sure you'll get one soon," Mona said. She sounded relieved.

"I don't really think so," Ashleigh said with a sigh. "I'm about to give up." *I seem to be a lot better at losing horses than getting them,* she thought.

"Ashleigh, we're ready to go!" Mr. Griffen called from the doorway to the house.

"Where are you going?" Mona asked.

"To look at a broodmare." Ashleigh frowned. Normally she would have been the first in the truck. But right then she didn't feel like doing anything.

"You'd better go talk to your parents," Mona said, quickly remounting. "I'll see you later."

She couldn't have been more obvious about wanting to

get her precious horse away from me, Ashleigh thought as she trudged to the house. *Some friend*. She banged the front door to the house behind her.

"There you are, sweetie," said Mrs. Griffen. "Were you riding Mona's horse?"

"For about a second." Ashleigh shrugged.

"Let's go see the Dansons' mare," Mr. Griffen said.

"I changed my mind. I just want to stay here." Ashleigh flopped onto the couch in the living room and picked up a horse magazine.

Her dad looked surprised. "Are you sure? This is a beautiful mare. I think you might be interested in seeing her."

Ashleigh shook her head. "I'd rather read."

Her parents exchanged looks. "Well, all right," Mrs. Griffen said. "I guess we can't convince you. But I think you'll be sorry you didn't go."

Ashleigh glanced out the window. "Why are you taking the trailer?" she asked her dad. "I thought you were just going to look at the mare."

"We'll take it along in case we decide to close the deal," Mr. Griffen said. "This mare looks pretty good."

Ashleigh was surprised. Her parents seldom closed deals on the spot. Usually they looked, then came home and talked over the prospect. But they seemed strangely excited about this horse.

"Ashleigh, why don't you get a stall ready in case we bring the mare back with us?" her mother asked.

"Okay." Ashleigh yawned. She guessed she didn't really feel like sitting inside all day. "What's her name?"

Mrs. Griffen was half out the door. "Stardust," she called back.

"That's a pretty name," Ashleigh murmured, leafing through her magazine.

After her parents left, she tossed the magazine aside and wandered out to the barn to decide where she should put the new horse.

"I'll put her at the end, so she won't be near Gallantry," Ashleigh said aloud, grabbing a couple of sheaves of straw out of the feed room. "If the new horse sees how Gallantry acts, she may not like it here, either." Gallantry was still a handful, even after weeks on the farm, away from the track. Ashleigh's parents sometimes tried to look at Gallantry's wild behavior optimistically—she might pass on all that spirit and fire to her foals. But mostly, Ashleigh knew, they were just tired of constantly repairing the stall and struggling with her.

Ashleigh scattered the straw and fluffed it up with a pitchfork. Then she filled a water bucket and looked around the stall one last time. It was all ready for the new horse, if she came. Ashleigh sighed. This empty stall reminded her of another empty one—Sunstorm's.

I wish I could get in a better mood, she thought. *Maybe I'll go spend some time with the horses.* Ashleigh stuffed her pockets with carrots from the stash in the feed room and headed outside.

In the back paddock most of the mares were looking straight at her, not grazing. The grass was winter brown and not very tempting, Ashleigh supposed. Besides, they probably didn't want to move. Go Gen was due to foal any day now, and almost all the mares would deliver over the next two months. Ashleigh felt a tickle of excitement at the thought of the births and the small foals flicking their tiny tails and wobbling on spindly legs as they explored the world.

Wanderer walked slowly over to the fence and sniffed Ashleigh's pockets.

"You look almost skinny compared to the rest of the mares," Ashleigh said, stroking Wanderer's satiny black neck. Ashleigh's parents had only succeeded in breeding Wanderer the past summer. That was very late in the season, but Wanderer was a blue hen, a mare that gave birth to a large number of high-quality foals, and so Ashleigh's parents had continued trying to breed her to a well-known stallion. On the third try they had succeeded, but this foal would be the latest to be born of all the foals at Edgardale. Wanderer was expecting in June.

"Are you going to have a colt or a filly this year?" Ashleigh asked. Wanderer gently pulled a carrot out of her pocket and crunched it. "You always have first a colt, then a filly, so I guess this year you'll have a colt. I wonder what he'll be like?"

Wanderer nudged her pocket, asking for more carrots.

"I know, June's a long way off. We'll wait and see." Ashleigh smiled.

She looked at the other mares. They stayed where they were, even though by now they had seen that Ashleigh had carrots. "Not worth it to move, huh?" she said. "You guys *are* close to having your foals if you'll pass up a chance at carrots."

Finally Ashleigh took pity on them and brought the carrots out to everybody. The mares munched, looking grateful, she thought. It was nice to know that they were hardly ever sold.

Ashleigh stepped back and climbed on top of the fence. The air was nippy and the sky cloudy, but she loved watching the horses. In the paddock next door the yearlings were playing games, pushing each other and frolicking up and down the fence line.

I feel okay now, Ashleigh realized. *Maybe in the spring I'll work with some of the other yearlings, like Jill-in-the-Box and Moon Bright.*

About an hour later Ashleigh heard the truck and trailer coming up the driveway. Her father parked the rig in front of the barn and swung out of the cab. Ashleigh hurried over and looked in the back of the trailer. There was definitely a horse in there, although she couldn't see much of it in the evening light. "You bought Stardust!" she said excitedly.

"We're trying her out," Mr. Griffen said mysteriously. "We want to see how she handles."

Ashleigh wondered why. Broodmares didn't have to be stars at equitation. Mostly they just had to be healthy and have good pedigrees.

"Ashleigh, would you mind exercising Stardust?" Mrs. Griffen asked. "I think you'll enjoy riding her. She's part Thoroughbred—her owners say she's fast."

"Great!" Ashleigh couldn't believe her luck. This day was ending so much better than it had started! She grabbed a lead line from the fence and hurried back to the

127

trailer. Suddenly she stopped dead. "If she's only part Thoroughbred, why are we buying her?"

Her parents looked at each other. "Well, actually, her owners may give her to a girl about your age."

This gets weirder and weirder, Ashleigh thought. She wasn't going to waste time questioning her parents, though—it was getting dark. "What do you want me to do with her?" Ashleigh asked.

"Just about anything you want. She's fairly well conditioned—one of the grooms has been riding her at the Dansons'. If you feel like it, a good gallop might be just the thing for her," Mrs. Griffen said.

Ashleigh smiled. She definitely felt like taking a good gallop.

"Stardust's tack is in the front compartment of the trailer. I'll bring her out," Mr. Griffen said.

Ashleigh opened the compartment and lifted out an English saddle and bridle. They were of good quality, and the slightly worn leather was soft and supple. She carried the tack to the back of the trailer. Her father opened the trailer doors and began guiding Stardust out.

Ashleigh stopped dead. The beautiful horse backing out of the trailer wasn't just any horse. It was the horse of her dreams!

Stardust was a copper-colored chestnut, with a flowing darker mane and tail. She hopped off the end of the trailer ramp and looked around. When she saw Ashleigh, she whickered softly.

"Hi, girl!" Ashleigh whispered. Hardly believing she was real, Ashleigh ran her hand over Stardust's silky neck.

Then she walked slowly around the mare. Stardust had two white stockings on her hind legs and a small white star. She was on the small side—Ashleigh guessed a little under fifteen hands—but she had beautiful conformation.

"What do you think?" Mr. Griffen asked, smiling.

Ashleigh could hardly talk. "She's gorgeous!"

"Why don't you tack Stardust up right here and get started on your ride?" Mrs. Griffen said. "We already groomed her at the Dansons'."

Ashleigh quickly saddled and bridled Stardust. The mare stood quietly, then looked back at her and whickered throatily. Ashleigh tried not to pay attention. *She's not your horse,* she reminded herself. *Don't fall in love with her. She's going to disappear a lot quicker than Sunstorm did.*

Ashleigh swung easily into the saddle. Stardust danced in place, eager to be off.

"Have fun," called Mrs. Griffen.

"We will." Ashleigh waved and squeezed with her legs, asking Stardust to walk toward the lane. The mare responded instantly.

"Nobody told me you would look like this, Stardust," Ashleigh said. "I almost wish you didn't. I'd like you to stay."

Stardust's ears flicked back. "You listen to everything I say, don't you?" Ashleigh smiled. "Somebody must have loved you and talked to you all the time."

As they reached the lane a fine drizzle began to fall. "Should we go back?" Ashleigh asked. "I don't mind the rain if you don't. I'd like to ride you, even if it's just this once."

Stardust shook her head, sending a spray of droplets from her mane.

"Good. Let's go on." Ashleigh turned up her face, letting the soft rain settle on it. She liked the feel of the cold mist on her face and hair. She'd freeze if the rain got heavier, but so far riding was keeping her warm.

Ashleigh looked between Stardust's small, finely shaped ears to the lane ahead. Stardust effortlessly covered the ground. Her gaits were much more fluid than Ranger's.

"I wonder if it's too wet to gallop," Ashleigh said. "I bet it's not, really. Racehorses gallop in the mud all the time, and you're part Thoroughbred, Stardust."

Ashleigh glanced up at the sky. She didn't have to look far—the wispy gray clouds were almost on the ground. They were turning into fog. If she didn't gallop Stardust now, she might miss her chance—and it would be the last chance she ever got. "What do you think, girl?" she asked.

Stardust pawed the soft ground, pulling the reins through Ashleigh's fingers. "Let's do it," Ashleigh said. Before she could even signal Stardust, the mare moved effortlessly from a walk into a canter.

She understands what I want, Ashleigh thought. She leaned forward. "Go for it!" she cried.

The chestnut mare charged ahead at a gallop, her hooves throwing up clumps of mud as she dug for ground. Instinctively Ashleigh crouched over her horse's neck. Stardust's wet mane blew into her face, and she could hear the mare's muffled snorts as she pounded along, increasing her speed with every stride.

Ashleigh laughed aloud from sheer exuberance.

Stardust's strides were so smooth and fast, she barely seemed to touch the ground. They were flying!

If she were my horse, I'd do this every day, Ashleigh thought. *That would be so fantastic!*

Stardust whipped around a curve in the lane. Ashleigh felt the mare's hind legs slip a little. A flash of fear shot through her.

"No, Stardust!" she gasped, trying to ease up the mare with the reins. "Not so fast! You're *not* my horse. I don't know if you're used to gallops like this!"

At first Ashleigh thought Stardust wouldn't respond. The mare was in high gear, and she didn't want to stop running. Ashleigh didn't dare yank too hard on her and risk throwing her off balance on the slippery ground. Ashleigh pulled back hard on the reins again. She just had to stop her. This time Stardust reluctantly dropped back into a canter, and finally into a high-stepping, spirited trot.

Ashleigh's shoulders sagged with relief. *But I know why she didn't stop at first. She wasn't sure I really wanted her to,* Ashleigh thought.

Streamers of fog wrapped around them as she walked Stardust back to the stable, cooling her out. The fenceposts along the paddocks looked like pointing fingers wreathed in mist. Familiar as Ashleigh was with every inch of the farm, for a second she didn't know where they were.

"It's getting hard to see," she said to Stardust. "What if we got lost? Then we'd never have to go home. Maybe we're in an enchanted forest."

Stardust whickered, as if to say she'd like that, too.

Ashleigh half closed her eyes, breathing in the thick, moist air. The mud made soft sucking noises beneath Stardust's hooves. Stardust walked easily along, flicking back her ears, awaiting any instructions. In the growing dark her damp coat looked almost black. Ashleigh dreamed of riding Stardust on a sunny day through a meadow filled with flowers. The light would turn Stardust's coat to pure copper. They would race, faster than any other horse and rider could go, pounding across the grass.

Stardust stopped suddenly. "What is it, girl?" Ashleigh asked. Then she realized they had reached the stable yard fence. In the growing darkness, preoccupied with her thoughts, she hadn't realized they were back.

Now I have to get off and give Stardust to that other girl, Ashleigh thought miserably. *It isn't fair—Stardust and I are perfect together!*

Ashleigh opened the gate and led Stardust into the stable yard. By the time they reached the barn, the rain was coming down in buckets. Ashleigh put Stardust in crossties, then quickly took off the mare's tack and toweled her off. She put a warm blanket over her. "I don't want you to get chilled," she said. Stardust gave a soft nicker, as if in thanks.

Ashleigh stepped back to look at her. Even damp and with her mane bedraggled, Stardust was the most beautiful horse she'd ever seen.

"How was your ride?" Mr. Griffen asked. Her parents walked up from the office.

Ashleigh nodded. "All right." *Now they'll take her away,* she thought. She felt sick with disappointment.

"Just all right?" Mr. Griffen pressed.

"No," Ashleigh said. She knew her voice sounded funny. "It was the best ride I ever had."

"Then that's settled," Mrs. Griffen said. "What stall did you get ready for her?"

"She's spending the night? Are the new owners picking her up tomorrow?" Ashleigh asked.

"We're her owners," Mrs. Griffen said with a smile.

For a second Ashleigh couldn't believe she'd heard right. "You're buying Stardust?" she gasped.

Mr. Griffen nodded. "Actually, the Dansons are giving her away. Their youngest daughter is in college now, so no one is really riding Stardust anymore. The Dansons just want to find a good home for her. I told them I thought we could provide one."

Ashleigh rushed to Stardust and threw her arms around her neck. "Do you hear that? You're staying! Oh, this is so incredible!"

Stardust bent her head and blew gently in Ashleigh's hair. She seemed glad, too.

"Why didn't you tell me?" Ashleigh couldn't stop looking at Stardust—at *their* horse.

"We wanted to see if you suited each other first. I guess we found out you do." Mrs. Griffen smiled.

"Stardust will be yours in a year or so if you take good care of her and keep up your grades in school," Mr. Griffen said. "Do you think you can do that?"

"Of course I can!" Those were such small things to do to earn a horse of her own, Ashleigh thought. "Come on, girl," she said happily. "Let's get you settled in."

Stardust followed her eagerly to her stall. Ashleigh filled her hay net and feed bucket and stepped back as Stardust dug in. "Can you believe you're here?" she asked. "I can't!"

Ashleigh stayed in the barn a long time, admiring the mare. Stardust was just so exquisite, from her dark, prominent eyes to her polished black hooves.

"Dinner, Ash!" Rory called. He pulled himself up on the stall's half-door and hung over it to look in. "Wow, is that your new horse?"

"Yes—this is Stardust," Ashleigh said proudly. The mare left her hay net to sniff Rory for a second, then returned to her dinner.

"She's pretty." Rory studied the mare.

"I'll come up to the house in a while," Ashleigh said. "I don't want to leave Stardust yet."

"You can see her tomorrow." Rory's face disappeared as he slid back down over the door. "Moe and I will ride with you!" he called.

Ashleigh smiled to herself. "That's right, I can see her tomorrow. She'll always be here from now on." She opened the stall door and gave Stardust a final pat. "Sleep well, girl. We'll go for another fantastic ride tomorrow!"

13

"So I heard Edgardale didn't do too badly at Keeneland," Diana said casually to Ashleigh the next Tuesday at Chesterton. Diana propped her elbows on the door to Ranger's stall.

Ashleigh stopped brushing Ranger and looked at Diana warily. She still wasn't sure if Diana's niceness about Caroline had been a fluke. Diana might be about to play a trick. "Edgardale did great at the auction. So what?"

Ranger pricked his ears and sidestepped away from Diana. Ashleigh wondered if Diana had already done something to him that day. "Easy, boy," Ashleigh murmured. "Yeah," she said to Diana, turning back to her grooming. "Our colt was one of the highest-priced yearlings at the sale. I guess you could call that not doing too badly."

Diana didn't say anything for a few moments. Ashleigh continued to brush Ranger, making careful, deep circles with the rubber currycomb. Ranger's ears relaxed, and he sighed with enjoyment.

"Well, everybody in Louisville heard about it." Diana hesitated. "You were there, right?"

"Yup." Ashleigh knelt to examine Ranger's knees. They seemed completely healed, although she could still see the scars.

"Didn't you get your own horse, too?"

"How did you know?"

"Your mom told Jane." Ashleigh knew her mother had called Jane to find out if Ranger was well enough to be ridden. "Are you going to bring your horse to the lessons?" Diana asked.

"Not right away. Jane thinks it's better if I learn on a school horse. That way we won't both be learning." Ashleigh felt a momentary stab at being away from Stardust. They'd gone on another wonderful ride the day before. The ground had dried up, and they'd gone even faster than they had the first day.

Ashleigh wished she could show off her beautiful horse at the lessons. She hadn't even shown her to Mona yet, because Mona had had a dentist's appointment the day before. They'd arranged to ride the next day for sure.

I wish I were home riding my own horse instead of here, Ashleigh thought. She wouldn't get to ride Stardust at all that day. It would be dark by the time she got home.

"You could come out with us for ice cream after the riding lesson," Diana suggested. "Barbara's dad usually takes us."

Ashleigh glanced over at her in surprise. She and Diana barely spoke to each other, much less hung out together.

"Caroline can come, too. But wait, she's not here, is she?" Diana asked.

"No, the doctor doesn't want her to ride yet." Ashleigh didn't add that Caroline didn't seem to care at all about riding anymore.

"We can celebrate your good luck at the auction by eating ice cream," Diana said.

Oh, I get it, Ashleigh thought. *My family made a lot of money at the auction and I have my own horse, so now Diana thinks I'm good enough to hang out with.* "It wasn't just luck that Sunstorm brought a high price at the auction. He's a great horse." Ashleigh stopped brushing. "Thanks for the offer, but I have to go home right after the lesson and help with our horses."

Diana made a face. "I guess that's the bad part about having a farm."

"Nope—it's the good part. I love taking care of them." Ashleigh picked up one of Ranger's hooves.

"If you say so." Diana shrugged. "Talk to you later."

Ranger swung his head around quickly, ears pricked. "Yes, she's gone," Ashleigh said. "I don't trust her, either."

"Hi, Ashleigh!" Barbara called over the stall door on her way down the aisle.

"Hi." Ashleigh looked at Ranger. The gelding had relaxed now that Diana was gone. He was standing on three legs, with his eyes half closed. "Guess what, boy? I'm so lucky. Now all the snobs like me."

Ranger closed his eyes all the way, as if he were completely unimpressed. Ashleigh laughed and quickly tacked him up.

Just before she led him into the ring, she checked the girth. It was loose. "Bad guy," Ashleigh scolded. "I thought maybe you'd forget some of your tricks when you got hurt. But I guess not, huh?" She pulled up the girth by two notches.

Ranger laid back his ears a fraction.

"Tough if you don't like it. That saddle's staying on today." Ashleigh mounted. Ranger snorted, but his ears flicked forward.

Ashleigh circled Ranger at a walk, looking for any sign that he was favoring one of his front legs, but his injuries appeared to have healed well. Ranger stepped out briskly. He seemed glad to be out of his stall. "You seem okay, thank goodness," Ashleigh said. "We all recovered pretty well from that accident—except I don't know if Caroline will ever come near a horse again."

Diana trotted over on Silverado. "We started jumping while you were gone," she said. Ashleigh noticed that a grid of cavalletti and several low crossbars and parallels was set up around the ring. "Want me to explain what we did?" Diana offered. "We've got a few minutes before class starts. Jane isn't even here."

Diana really is trying to be nice, Ashleigh thought. She decided to give her a chance. "Okay," she said. "But Ranger and I know how to jump already. We took a huge jump going after Caroline when Neptune ran away with her. I went back and looked at it the next day, when the snow melted. It was a rock about three feet high. If Ranger had missed, he'd be dead now."

"Jeez. I don't know if Jane wants Ranger to jump yet,

since his knees got messed up," Diana said. "You can ride Silverado if you want. We'll take turns."

"Thanks." Ashleigh was surprised that Diana would let her ride her valuable horse. Mona had been so stingy about letting her ride Frisky, and Frisky wasn't worth half what Silverado was.

"Okay, class, listen up!" Jane strode into the ring. "Today we'll work on jumps again. Form a line and warm up over the cavalletti at a trot. Then we'll take it one at a time over the course." She smiled at Ashleigh. "Welcome back."

Ashleigh smiled back. "Thanks."

"I told Ashleigh she could ride Silverado over the jumps, since Ranger can't do them yet," Diana said.

"Thank you, Diana." Jane looked slightly shocked.

No wonder, Ashleigh thought. *Jane would have to be blind not to know who's been playing all the tricks on me at the stable since I started taking lessons here.*

"I'm sure a few times over the cavalletti will be enough for you to catch up," Jane said to Ashleigh. "Let's get started. Diana, you first, then you girls can trade off horses."

Diana circled at a trot, then pointed Silverado at the cavalletti. The big gray horse trotted through the grid, but Diana took him in at an angle over the last two poles. He had to hop awkwardly over them.

"Straighten him out next time, Diana!" Jane yelled. "Fix your angle on the jumps before you take them, as you're coming out of the circle. And eyes up! Bring him through again after Barbara and Cheryl."

Diana got at the back of the line. After the other horses in the class had gone through, she tried again. Silverado still went in at an angle.

This time Jane didn't say anything about Diana's performance. Ashleigh wondered if Jane had given up on Diana. Ashleigh was anxious for her turn on Silverado. If she could believe Diana's bragging, he was a world-class jumper.

"Now you try, Ashleigh," Jane said. Diana rode Silverado over to Ashleigh, dismounted, and handed her his reins. "Have fun," she said.

"I will." Ashleigh gave Ranger's reins to Diana. Ashleigh wondered briefly if when she came back, Ranger would have a burr under his saddle or Diana would have done something else to him. But maybe she and Diana were friends now.

Ashleigh had to lower the stirrup to get on Silverado. He was a very tall horse, well over sixteen hands. Once mounted, she walked him up and down the side of the ring, getting used to the feel of her seat and hands with him. Silverado instantly responded to the slightest touch of the reins or shift in weight.

"You really are a great horse," Ashleigh murmured.

"Ready?" Jane called.

Ashleigh turned Silverado and trotted him to the far end of the ring. She circled him in preparation for the jumps and focused ahead. Silverado flawlessly took the cavalletti. His gaits were so smooth, riding him felt like butter.

"Good!" Jane said. "Okay, everyone, let's go on to the crossrails and parallels."

"You can go first," Diana said when Ashleigh rode Silverado over to her at the rail. Ashleigh saw that somehow Diana had gotten a soda from the machine inside the tack room, even though she was holding Ranger.

"Did you tie him to the rail while you got that?" Ashleigh asked accusingly. She knew Diana couldn't have taken Ranger with her into the tack room, but a horse tied by the bridle could severely injure its mouth.

"Just for a second." Diana shrugged. "Don't have a cow. You sound like Jane."

"It would have taken only a second for him to get hurt if he spooked or something, poor guy." Ashleigh didn't want Ranger to get injured just when his knees had healed up. *It's rough being a school horse,* she thought.

"The key to jumping is in the approach," Jane was saying as Ashleigh and Silverado rejoined the class. "Once your approach is correct, you're generally in good shape for the jump. So you want to start planning your approach long in advance. Cheryl, take Dynasty around the course in the following order: parallel, crossbar, two parallels." Jane pointed to the jumps.

Cheryl circled Dynasty. He was so big, Ashleigh thought Cheryl looked as though she were posting in slow motion. She pointed him at the first jump.

"Don't glue your eyes to the ground! Look up at the bleachers!" Jane yelled.

Cheryl finally looked up, but Dynasty stumbled going into the crossbar and took it down.

Ashleigh saw why. Cheryl hadn't planned the approach

until Dynasty was right on top of the jump. Because of the horse's speed at a canter, she hadn't had time to collect him. Now both horse and rider were rattled. Dynasty took down both of the last two parallels as well.

"Way to go," Diana called. "You almost got a hundred percent—down."

Cheryl flushed.

Her horse is just too big for her, Ashleigh thought. *I don't care how much he cost. She can't control him.*

"Ashleigh, you go," Jane said. She sounded weary. "Remember what I said about approach."

Ashleigh nodded and squeezed with her legs, signaling Silverado to trot. As they approached the jump Ashleigh had him headed in straight. She tried to estimate how many strides he should take before he lifted off. She wasn't sure—one more or two? If he took two, the second one would be very short. Ashleigh squeezed again with her legs and leaned forward.

That was wrong! she thought with alarm the instant they lifted off. Silverado responded to her command and jumped, but he had to make a huge leap. Ashleigh quickly leaned forward, helping the gelding as much as she could. Still Silverado ticked the pole with his hind legs. They hit the ground jarringly. Ashleigh was thrown back in the saddle and accidentally pulled hard on his mouth. Silverado threw up his head, and Ashleigh barely recovered her seat. "Sorry, boy," she said, stroking his neck as soon as she could. "You did what I asked, but it just didn't work, did it?"

"Nope," Jane called, as if she had heard.

"I know." Ashleigh glanced over at Diana to see if she was upset. Diana was talking and laughing with her friends. She wasn't paying attention at all.

"That's good," Ashleigh muttered to herself. "She won't be mad about what I did to her horse."

"Try that again," Jane said. "Shorten up on the reins and keep him collected over the jump. Even though Silverado is an experienced jumper, he needs guidance."

The next time around, Ashleigh adjusted her reins to shorten Silverado's stride. They sailed gracefully over the jump.

"Very pretty." Jane nodded.

"That felt right," Ashleigh said. "You're an incredible jumper, Silver!" But she wasn't having as much fun as she did racing Stardust along the lanes at Edgardale. Ashleigh remembered again the only jump she'd taken before this one—her wild leap over the rock after Caroline and Neptune. *Maybe I'd like jumping more if I'd tried it some other way first,* she thought.

She rode Silverado over to Diana. "Your turn," she said. "I'm sorry I yanked on him the first time around."

Diana looked surprised, then she shrugged. "He'll live," she said.

Diana doesn't care if her horse's training gets messed up, Ashleigh thought as Diana circled before the jump course. *That's why she let me ride him. She isn't really nicer than Mona.*

Ashleigh watched Diana take Silverado over the jumps. Now that Ashleigh had ridden him, she could see that Diana was mostly just a passenger. Silverado was deciding what they would do and how they would do it. Because he was so highly trained, usually he got it exactly right.

After the lesson Ashleigh hurried Ranger back to his stall and lightly groomed him. She was anxious to get home to Stardust, whom she'd barely had time to say hello to after school. She tossed Ranger's brushes in his box and opened the stall door. Ranger nudged her hard. He seemed to be looking at her reproachfully.

"Oh, I'm sorry," Ashleigh said. "You really are a good old boy, aren't you? You deserve a better brushing than that." She picked up the dandy brush again. Ranger bobbed his head, as if to say, *Now you've got the right idea.*

Diana looked over the half-door. "You looked good on Silver," she said. "But you don't even have to try, do you?"

"I have to pay attention. You don't have to try very hard, either." Ashleigh felt uncomfortable. Diana had been mad at her for months because Ashleigh was a better rider. Ashleigh didn't want to bring that up again just when they seemed to be getting along.

"Oh, I don't have to worry about trying because my horse is so good. I know that," Diana said. "*You're* really good."

"Thanks." Ashleigh looked over at Diana, wondering if she was going to get mad again. "You could be better if you worked at it," she said.

"Yeah, I guess, but I don't really want to. What's the point?" Diana unwrapped a stick of gum.

Ashleigh opened her mouth, then closed it. She didn't

know how anyone could stand not to look good on a horse. "Don't you like jumping?" she asked.

"It's okay." Diana shrugged. "Do you?"

"Not that much," Ashleigh said honestly. "Maybe it's because we're just beginning in the class. And steeplechasing and eventing are probably more exciting than stadium jumping."

"What does your horse at home do?" Diana asked.

"I'm not really sure yet." Ashleigh frowned in thought. "But she's fast. That's what I like to do most of all—ride fast, and work with our young horses."

"It must be fun to be in a family where everyone really cares about horses. Mine doesn't," Diana said. "My father expects me to be the best in the class, but he hardly ever watches me ride. He just grills Jane about how I'm doing, and she says awful."

"She does not."

"She says I have an awful attitude."

"Maybe she doesn't think you try hard." Ashleigh combed Ranger's tail.

"I don't."

"Then it's not going to work, Diana." Ashleigh straightened up and looked at her. "You can't expect to be a good rider if you don't try hard."

Diana shrugged again. "Oh, well."

Ashleigh looked around Ranger's stall. He had fresh water, a full hay net, and a thick pile of clean straw to rest on. "I'm done," she said. "I've got to go."

"So can you come out with us tonight?" Diana asked. "We could pick you up after you finish your chores."

"I can't. I have to baby-sit my little brother," Ashleigh said, giving Ranger a last pat. "My parents are going to dinner with some other owners of breeding farms. They don't want Caroline to have to look after Rory and get stressed out. She's still supposed to go to bed early."

"You're lucky to have a brother and sister." Diana looked wistful.

"I am?" Ashleigh laughed. "You get to stay here as long as you want and ride your incredible horse. I have to chase a five-year-old all over the house, clean up his sticky messes, and play with his GI Joes. And I have to share a room with Caroline. She's always yelling at me to pick up my junk."

Diana just leaned on Ranger's door.

"Aren't you leaving?" Ashleigh asked. "You hang out here a lot."

"I may spend the night here," Diana muttered.

"Doesn't sound so bad." Ashleigh set her dandy brush in Ranger's box.

"You don't get it." Diana looked away. "I don't have anywhere else to go. I'm an only child, and my mom is sick."

"That's really tough," Ashleigh said.

"Oh, I guess I'm used to it most of the time." Diana kicked the stall door. "But I like being here with the horses better than being anywhere else."

I can understand that, Ashleigh thought. "You could come home with me," she said.

"Thanks. I guess I'll go get ice cream with my friends. It does help to have friends." Diana smiled weakly.

Ashleigh smiled back. She felt sorry for Diana. "Yeah, it does," she agreed. *It's funny, but I guess we're kind of friends now,* she thought. "Thanks for letting me ride Silver," she said. "He's such a great horse."

"Yeah." Diana pushed herself off the stall door. "Well, catch you later."

Ranger stuck his head over the door and watched Diana go. He pricked his ears.

"It's okay, boy," Ashleigh said, rubbing his blaze. "We don't need to worry about her anymore."

14

ASHLEIGH WALKED UP THE STAIRS AFTER SCHOOL THE NEXT day to change clothes. She planned to go for a dynamite ride on Stardust. There was so much she and the mare hadn't done yet. Stardust hadn't been to the woods or the creek, or met Frisky.

Caroline was lying on her bed, reading a teen magazine. "Do you want to go for a ride?" Ashleigh asked. *Say yes today,* she hoped. Since Caroline had gotten home from the hospital, she hadn't wanted to ride. She didn't even seem to want to be around the horses anymore.

But Ashleigh was sure that someday Caroline would want to ride with her again. Especially now that they had Stardust! "We can take turns on Stardust," she offered. "Or you can ride her and I'll take Moe."

Caroline yawned and stretched. "I don't think so, Ash. I looked at her yesterday, and she's beautiful. But I'm pretty comfortable here. And I don't really want to try out a new horse."

"You could ride Moe," Ashleigh said. *I have to get Caroline to ride again,* she thought. *She can't be really happy if she isn't around horses.*

Caroline laughed. "Moe's more dangerous than any other horse in the world! He always tries to run away."

"So you don't want to ride at all now." Ashleigh sat down on the end of her sister's bed. "Do you hate horses?" she asked seriously.

"No, of course not. But I've had enough of riding for a while." Caroline smiled wryly. "Don't worry. I'm not mad at Neptune or anything. I might ride again someday, but not now. Besides, I've got so much schoolwork to make up, I really don't have time."

"You could do homework after we ride a little," Ashleigh argued. "We could—"

Mrs. Griffen looked in the door. "Ashleigh, may I speak to you for a minute? Come on downstairs."

Ashleigh quickly changed into a T-shirt and old jeans and ran down the stairs after her mother. *Caroline's changed so much since she fell,* Ashleigh thought. Her sister had always liked to spend time inside, doing things such as reading, watching old movies, and fooling around with makeup and hairstyles. But now she almost never left the house. For the first few weeks Ashleigh had thought her sister just didn't feel good, but Caroline had returned to school and the doctor had given her a clean bill of health.

"Come on in the kitchen," Mrs. Griffen called.

"What?" Ashleigh asked, walking into the kitchen and taking a carton of strawberry yogurt out of the refrigerator.

"Sweetie, I know you mean well when you ask Caroline to ride again, but I just don't want you to push it," Mrs. Griffen said.

"When you fall off a horse, you're supposed to get right back on," Ashleigh argued. "Otherwise you'll always be scared to. I know Caro couldn't get back on earlier because she was hurt, but shouldn't she try now?"

"Caroline may not be completely well yet." Mrs. Griffen sighed. "Even when she is, I'm just not sure she belongs on a horse. Maybe when she's older, I'll feel differently."

"She's not going to have much fun if she can't ride," Ashleigh said.

Mrs. Griffen smiled. "You and I think that, but it's not true for everybody. Some people can't really control a horse. And those people aren't going to have fun riding—they're going to get hurt. Even you have to be careful on a horse and not do anything reckless, Ashleigh, but no matter how careful Caroline is, she still might lose control."

"I'm sorry I tried to make her ride," Ashleigh said slowly. She felt bad that she had pressured Caroline to do something that might be dangerous for her. "I just wanted to help."

"I know you did." Mrs. Griffen squeezed Ashleigh's shoulders. "I'm sure Caroline was pleased you want to be with her so much."

"Well, I think I'll ride with Mona," Ashleigh said. She had already arranged to meet her friend. Ashleigh guessed she'd already known in her heart that Caroline wouldn't be coming with her.

"Okay." Mrs. Griffen smiled. "I put Stardust up for you in the barn so that she'd be ready to go. Somehow I had a feeling that you were going to ride today."

"I sure am." Ashleigh quickly spooned up the rest of her yogurt and hurried to the barn. Stardust was looking out of her stall, tossing her elegant head. Ashleigh could feel her mood lightening the second she saw her.

"Are you waiting for me?" Ashleigh called. This was almost too good to be true—her very own gorgeous horse, right in a stall at Edgardale! No more pretending other horses were hers on brief rides or dreaming about owning a horse!

Stardust bent farther over the door to put her head in Ashleigh's arms.

"I was afraid you wouldn't be here," she murmured. "I wasn't sure you were real."

Stardust nudged her firmly, and Ashleigh laughed. "I guess you wish I would quit talking and ride you! Okay, let's go!"

She quickly brought the mare out to the crossties and groomed her. Stardust's coat shone like a bright new penny, and her mane and tail flowed like copper silk.

"I've never seen a more beautiful horse than you," Ashleigh said. "I wouldn't mind staying in here another hour, just looking at you. But I think Mona's probably waiting for us by now."

Stardust whickered and stamped her foot. After casting one last glance over her horse, Ashleigh got Stardust's saddle and bridle from the tack room. She spent a little more time admiring how the mare looked under saddle, then quickly mounted and rode through the stable yard.

The days were lengthening as spring approached, so now Ashleigh could get in a good two-hour ride after school. She posted easily down the lane, enjoying the pungent, earthy smell of the wet ground. All the snow had melted. The bare branches of the trees and the stiff brown grass seemed to be waiting for the first hint of spring warmth.

Mona cantered Frisky down the lane. "Stardust's so gorgeous! Isn't it amazing that we've both got our own horses?" she asked with a broad smile.

"It's too fantastic." Ashleigh couldn't stop smiling. "And we're about to take our first ride! Well, Stardust isn't exactly mine, but she almost is. I have to show my parents I can take care of her and do well in school before she'll really be mine and not just my parents'."

"No problem!" Mona said.

"Right." Ashleigh grinned. "Let's go!"

As they cantered up the lane Ashleigh couldn't help comparing the two horses. Frisky was a little taller, since she was all Thoroughbred and Stardust was only part. Frisky had been a handful when Ashleigh tried to ride her, but now she was going along quietly. Her personality in general seemed quieter, like Mona's.

Maybe Frisky and I really weren't right for each other, she thought. *We didn't click the way Stardust and I do.*

The girls slowed the horses to a walk at the edge of the woods. Stardust looked around at the gray and black trees and brown grass of the winter landscape, flicking her ears with interest.

"You like being out, don't you?" Ashleigh asked. "Well, don't worry—we'll be riding every day it isn't sleeting. Maybe even then." She looked between Stardust's small, well-shaped ears. "I'd just need to get Stardust some kind of hat."

"It didn't sleet here all winter," Mona said.

"Then I guess we really will be out every day, huh, girl?" Ashleigh smiled with sheer pleasure at the prospect.

Ashleigh saw a foot-high log across the path. *I'll bet we could jump that,* she thought. She reined Stardust in.

"What do you think?" she asked the mare. "Are you a jumper? Probably you haven't been trained as one, or my parents would have told me."

Stardust pawed the ground. She seemed to understand what Ashleigh wanted.

Mona rode up next to them on Frisky. "Are you going to jump that?" she asked.

"I don't know." Something was holding Ashleigh back. She had a very clear memory of Ranger's incredible jump over the huge, snow-covered mound as they rushed to rescue Caroline—and her horror when she saw the size of the bare rock the next day. If Ranger hadn't been a trained jumper, the rescue would probably have ended in disaster.

But Stardust was so much smarter and more willing than Ranger. Ashleigh stared at the log. It was almost irresistible.

Then she remembered her talk with her mother. Being a little careful couldn't hurt. "I won't try it," she said, reluctantly turning Stardust to walk around the log. "We don't really know how to jump. And I don't want anything to happen to Stardust, ever."

"It won't," Mona said. "Let's canter!"

Ashleigh squeezed with her legs, and Stardust charged into the faster gait. Stardust's quick, smooth strides ate up the ground. Ashleigh leaned back, loving the feel of the damp, chilly air on her face and the power of the horse beneath her. Mona and Frisky thundered after her.

At last, breathless, they pulled the horses up at the edge of Edgardale. They looked at each other and laughed. "That was wonderful!" Mona said.

"Incredible." Ashleigh bent to press her cheek against Stardust's warm neck.

"We're going to be in fantastic shape if we do this every day," Mona said.

"Yeah, especially since I still have my lessons," Ashleigh said. "I've got one on Saturday. I guess I'll be riding Diana's horse again for jumping, if Ranger still can't jump."

"Wow! Diana lets you ride her million-dollar horse?" Mona asked. "So you guys must be friends. I noticed all the kids in Diana's gang are being nice to you at school."

"I don't think we're really friends." Ashleigh shook her head. "I'm glad she isn't mad at me anymore. But I don't want to be friends with somebody who's nice only if I have money and my own horse."

"I thought she was jealous of you because you're a

154

better rider," Mona said. "It's going to get even worse if you take Stardust to the lessons!"

"I guess I'll take Stardust sometime, but not until I learn to jump better." *It would be fun to show off my horse,* she thought. *But I don't know if I want to take her over to Chesterton and trot her around the ring. It's a lot more fun riding here.*

"Let's gallop!" she said.

"Okay—where to?" Mona asked.

"To the very end of the lane. That's about three miles. I think Stardust's in good enough shape. She was barely winded when I galloped her a mile the other day."

"I think Frisky's in good shape, too," Mona said.

Ashleigh signaled Stardust to canter. The mare jumped out into the quick, rocking gait. Then on her own Stardust shifted into a gallop, her hooves digging into the ground. Almost without thinking, Ashleigh leaned forward. They began to draw away from Mona and Frisky.

"Ashleigh, let's not really race!" Mona called.

"Why?" Ashleigh asked.

"Let's wait a little longer. We just got our horses. If we go really fast, they might run off with us. Let's try a slow gallop, then race the next time."

"Okay," Ashleigh said reluctantly. "We won't let them out all the way. But that doesn't mean Stardust and I won't beat you home! Come on, girl!"

15

In front of the gate at Chesterton the next Saturday, Ashleigh saw Diana climbing out of her father's Porsche. Her face was flushed.

"Hi," Ashleigh said, opening the gate.

"Hi. Could you give me a ride home?" Diana asked abruptly as they walked toward the barn.

"You mean right now?" Ashleigh said in surprise. Diana seemed really upset.

"No—after the lesson. My dad just told me he's too busy to come get me. He has to go to a business meeting. I guess if no one can take me home, I'm supposed to walk ten miles."

"Don't worry about it," Ashleigh said quickly. "You can get a ride with us."

"He didn't have to scream at me," Diana muttered as they walked into the barn. "Oh—you can jump Silver today if you want."

"Thanks. I'll ask Jane how Ranger is." Ashleigh stopped by the stable office. Jane sat at a metal desk, writing on a show entry form.

"How's Ranger?" Ashleigh asked.

Jane looked up from her paperwork. "He seems fine. I don't recommend that we run him in steeplechases, but I think he can handle the two-foot jumps in our class. Let's give it a try."

"Great!" Ashleigh hurried to Ranger's stall. She realized that she'd missed riding him. Even if Silverado was classier, she knew Ranger better and had a much stronger bond with him.

Ranger whinnied indignantly when he saw her. "I'm not going to neglect you today," Ashleigh said, opening the stall door. She led him to the crossties. "We let you rest for your own good."

Ranger stamped, as if he didn't believe her at all.

"Guess what—today we're going to try *tame* jumps," Ashleigh said. "This should be easy compared to the last time I jumped you."

Ashleigh quickly brushed Ranger and tacked him up, but she was still the last out to the ring again. Diana was trotting Silverado around.

Ashleigh stopped Ranger at the side of the ring to watch. Silverado's long, fluid strides effortlessly covered the ground. The gelding's silvery mane and tail flowed behind him like molten metal. In contrast, Diana slouched in the saddle, letting the reins sag.

She wouldn't ride badly on purpose, Ashleigh thought. *I guess she's still upset about her father.* Silverado had his

157

ears flicked back, listening. Diana's commands were sloppy, but the well-trained horse was still following every one of them.

"Okay, kids, line up for jumping," Jane said after they'd taken the horses through a walk, trot, and canter. "I moved the jumps around a little and raised the last one to two and a half feet, so be on your toes today. The horses may not be able to do them on automatic pilot. As the jumps get higher you'll see that there's less and less room for rider error. Okay, start us off, Diana."

Diana circled Silverado at a slow trot.

"Wake him up a little," Jane called.

Diana kicked Silverado hard. The gelding leaped forward as if he'd been stung. Diana checked him as she turned out of the circle to approach the jump.

"*Bring him in straight!*" Jane yelled.

Diana jerked on the reins, but she pulled too hard on the left one. Silverado obediently swerved left. Ashleigh saw Diana try to pull him straight, but going over the jump they almost hit the side pole.

"Let Ashleigh try him," Jane said abruptly.

Ashleigh winced. *I don't think showing off in front of Diana today is a good idea,* she thought. *She's already upset. But I guess I don't have a choice.* Ashleigh trotted Ranger over to Silverado.

Diana looked flushed and out of breath. She held out Silverado's reins. "Sorry," Ashleigh said.

"It's okay." Diana frowned. "It's not your fault—you have to ride him. If you don't, Jane will just yell more."

Ashleigh gathered Silverado's reins and adjusted her

stirrups. After an introductory circle she pointed him at the first jump. The gelding lifted over it with ease. Silverado floated over the rest of the jump course.

"You really do go like a dream," Ashleigh said, patting his neck.

Silver whuffed his pleasure at the kind words. *Poor guy,* Ashleigh thought. *I don't think Diana's very nice to you.*

"All right, Diana," Jane said. "Did you see how Ashleigh took the jumps? Now you try."

Diana slowly remounted Silverado. She sat for a second, slumped. Ashleigh wondered if for once Jane's words were getting through to her. Then Diana headed Silverado for the first jump.

He's short-striding, Ashleigh thought. *He's going to take off too close!*

"Diana, collect him! Don't let him bunny-hop!" Jane roared.

Diana yanked back hard on Silverado's mouth just as he was about to take off to jump. Then she booted him in the ribs.

"*No!*" Ashleigh gasped. Diana had asked Silver to jump and to stop at the same time. Ashleigh knew just what the highly trained horse would do. "*Don't pull him up like that!*" she yelled.

Silverado took off over the crossbar, but with very little momentum. For a second Ashleigh thought he would make the low jump. Then he seemed to freeze in midair. The next second he crashed down hard on the poles. Broken wood scattered as he fell, pinning Diana's leg under him. Her screams pierced the air.

Ashleigh galloped over to them just as Jane ran up. By the time they reached the fallen horse and rider, Silverado had rolled off Diana. He struggled to his feet, holding one hoof off the ground.

"Call an ambulance and the vet," Jane shouted at the other riders. "*Now!*"

Cheryl dismounted and ran out of the ring.

Jane knelt by Diana. Ashleigh rushed to Silverado's head. She saw to her horror that Silverado's leg was bent just above his ankle at an unnatural angle. "Jane, I think his leg is broken!" she said.

"Try to keep him still." Jane's voice was tense. "If he steps on it, he'll just injure it more. I'll help you as soon as we get Diana taken care of. *Be very careful*—he may lash out."

"Silver, take it easy, boy." Ashleigh tried to keep her voice from shaking.

At first the big horse seemed to be in shock. He tried to take a step, but the pain and Ashleigh's grip on the bridle stopped him. Ashleigh hung on desperately, praying she'd be able to hold him.

"Stand still, sweetie," Ashleigh said softly. "Just a little longer."

Silverado rolled his eyes to look at Ashleigh. The pain and fear in his eyes were almost too much for her to bear.

The stable vet, Dr. Sheldon, and the EMTs ran into the ring at the same time. Diana was quickly loaded onto a gurney and taken out the back door.

"I've got Silver on this side," Jane said, gripping the gelding's bridle. "Here comes help."

"Thank goodness," Ashleigh gasped. She could feel Silverado's muscles trembling. The next second he reared, throwing her into the air.

Ashleigh fell hard backward on her hands, but she scrambled to her feet and rushed to Silverado's side. She saw that Jane had fallen backward, too. Before either of them could reach Silverado, he tried to bolt. He landed on his broken leg with a sickening crunch of bone.

"No!" Ashleigh cried. The vet ran over to Silverado and grabbed his bridle.

"Talk to him," he said urgently. "You know him best. Say anything—I've got to tranquilize him, and I can't do that if he's thrashing around."

But I don't know him best, Ashleigh thought, panicking. What if they couldn't keep him still? "Good boy, Silver," she said. "You're such a good boy. Everything's going to be okay. . . ."

Finally the big horse responded for a moment. He lowered his head and stopped hauling against the restraint. But Ashleigh could feel that his muscles were still quivering.

Deftly Dr. Sheldon administered the shot into Silverado's neck. After a minute the big horse relaxed a little.

Good, now the vet can treat his leg, Ashleigh thought, looking down at it. She gasped in horror. The bone was sticking through the skin. Silverado had hurt his leg much more by walking on it.

"What do we do now?" Jane asked Dr. Sheldon. Her voice was taut.

"I'll probably operate," he said. "I'm putting on a temporary cast right now. This is a valuable horse. I don't want to destroy him if we've got another option."

Ashleigh closed her eyes for a second. "Does he have a good chance if you operate?" she asked.

The vet looked grim. "Maybe twenty percent."

Twenty percent! Ashleigh stared at him in disbelief. That couldn't be true. Silver couldn't just die.

"I hear the equine ambulance coming," Dr. Sheldon said. "Luckily, the veterinary hospital is close by."

The ambulance backed across the ring. Two attendants jumped out and opened the rear doors. The ambulance was equipped with a movable platform so that injured horses didn't have to step up to get inside.

Silverado stood on three legs, hanging his head. He still kept trying to put weight on the broken leg, now encased in the temporary cast. Gently Dr. Sheldon, Jane, and Ashleigh guided the injured horse into the ambulance.

"I'll ride over with him, Ashleigh," Jane said. "You go home."

"I guess I'll go back inside and look for my mother," Ashleigh said. She felt stunned. "She should be here by now."

"I'll let you know what happens," Jane said gently.

"Okay. Thanks." Ashleigh walked back into the stable. She could hear the horses quietly pulling hay from their nets and voices coming from the tack room. Ashleigh's boots echoed in the empty aisle as she walked quickly to Ranger's stall. She didn't want to talk to anybody.

Someone had put Ranger up for her. The chestnut

gelding looked away from his dinner long enough to whicker a greeting, then yanked another mouthful of hay from his net.

Ashleigh opened the door and put her arms around his neck. "Oh, Ranger," she said. "Now what? Silver has to make it. He just has to. He's too beautiful to die."

Ashleigh swallowed hard. She knew that vets could sometimes treat broken bones with drugs and surgery. But she remembered how badly Silverado's leg had been injured. It was hard not to think the worst.

She stepped out of the stall and walked to the barn door to look for her mother's car. She didn't see it on the drive. The night was overcast and very cold. Ashleigh shivered, even though she wore her down parka. *I wonder how Diana is*, she thought. *She must feel just terrible. I know I do.*

Ashleigh felt gentle hands on her shoulders. "How are you holding up?" Mrs. Griffen asked. "I heard what happened—Jane called me. I went over to the veterinary hospital first to look for you."

Ashleigh leaned into her mother's arms. "Oh, Mom, Silver knew how bad it was," she sobbed. "I could tell by the way he looked at me."

"It's not over yet," Mrs. Griffen said quietly. "Let's drive over to the hospital and find out how he is."

The waiting room at the hospital was brightly lit with harsh fluorescent lights. At the back were several doors. One of them was closed. Ashleigh knew the closed door must lead to the operating room.

Jane sat flipping through a magazine. She looked up when they walked in.

"What's the word?" Mrs. Griffen asked.

"Dr. Sheldon is still operating. We don't know yet. I did hear that Diana's okay—she's got a broken foot, but she'll mend. I wish I could say the same for Silverado." Jane tossed the magazine aside and buried her face in her hands.

"Don't blame yourself," Mrs. Griffen said.

"Oh, of course I do." Jane shook her head. "I didn't teach Diana right. If I had, this wouldn't have happened."

Ashleigh frowned. Jane hadn't taught Diana right, but that was because Diana wouldn't learn. "Diana had a fight with her dad before the lesson," she said. "That might be why she was having trouble."

"Well, I would have been hard on her even if I'd known," Jane said wearily. "She was riding badly. And this kind of injury is the result."

Ashleigh sat down next to Jane and tried to read a magazine. She couldn't concentrate on the words. Minutes, then hours, ticked by on the big wall clock.

Finally Dr. Sheldon walked out of the operating room. He ripped off his surgical gloves and threw them onto the counter.

Ashleigh felt a swelling bubble of fear in her chest. "How is he?" she asked.

"He went crazy coming out of the anesthetic. That's not an uncommon reaction. But he ripped off the cast." Dr. Sheldon's expression was grim. "He also injured his other foreleg thrashing around."

Jane groaned. Mrs. Griffen put her arm around Ashleigh.

"What will you do next?" Ashleigh asked. There had to be a way to help the injured horse.

"I did all I could," Dr. Sheldon said. He sounded very tired. "But I had no wish to prolong his agony. I put him down a minute ago."

Later that night Ashleigh stepped outside her house and looked up at the cold, black sky. It was still mostly overcast, and only a few weak stars twinkled dimly in between the clouds. Ashleigh wondered where Silverado was at that moment. It was so strange to think of him as being dead. He had been so full of life.

Dr. Sheldon had given Silverado a shot to put him out of his pain. Ashleigh knew that was the only thing the vet could have done, but it still hurt to think about it.

Ashleigh was so tired, she felt as though she were sleepwalking. But she doubted she would be able to sleep that night.

"Ashleigh?" Mr. Griffen looked out the door. "Are you all right?" He walked outside and stood beside Ashleigh, gazing at her with concern.

"I guess." Ashleigh swallowed. "But Dad—if only I could have done more for Silver. I couldn't hold him after he got hurt, and he broke away. . . ."

"Ashleigh, he was a twelve-hundred-pound horse," Mr. Griffen said. "You couldn't have done any better than you did."

"And Diana was so upset during the lesson because her father yelled at her," Ashleigh went on. "Maybe if I'd said something to cheer her up, she would have ridden better."

"Diana's got a lot of problems that have nothing to do with you," Mr. Griffen said. "You can't always stop terrible things from happening, sweetheart. You just have to do the best you can in a situation like that—which you did—and move on."

Ashleigh finally nodded. "I'm going to see Stardust," she said.

"Not now," Mr. Griffen said firmly. "Stardust will be waiting for you tomorrow, right in her stall. You've been outside enough for tonight. You look chilled to the bone."

Rory stuck his head under their father's arm and looked out the door. "Come on, Ash," he said. "Watch TV and eat popcorn with me and Caro. You'll feel better."

Ashleigh smiled at her little brother. "That sounds good. I'll try."

In school on Monday, Ashleigh sat by herself at lunch. Mona had a cold and had stayed home. Ashleigh didn't look for someone else to sit with. She still didn't feel much like talking to anyone.

Diana had hobbled into class that morning on her crutches, then sat down and gotten all her friends to sign her cast. She didn't seem to miss Silverado at all.

But Ashleigh did. She took an apple out of her lunch bag and took a bite. Then she set it down again. She wasn't hungry.

"Hi."

Ashleigh looked up and saw Diana. "Hi," she said. "Does it hurt?" She pointed to Diana's leg.

"Not much. I just have a hairline fracture. I shouldn't

have to wear this thing too long." Diana grimaced and touched her cast with a crutch.

"I'm really sorry about Silverado," Ashleigh said. Diana had to feel bad about her horse, even if she wasn't acting like it. "The vet worked a long time on him, but there wasn't anything he could do. I guess you heard about it."

"Yeah, Jane talked to my father. It doesn't matter that much." Diana shrugged. "My dad would get me a new horse if I wanted one."

Ashleigh's mouth dropped open in shock. Silverado's death didn't matter much? An incredibly valuable and talented horse had died because of Diana's carelessness, and that was all she had to say about it?

Diana saw Ashleigh's expression. "Look, horses just aren't that important to me. They're everything to you. I guess I'm not a bad rider. But the good thing about this is that I can quit riding. I've got soccer and a lot of other things to do."

"Would you still ride if I quit the lessons?" Ashleigh asked.

Diana looked at her for a moment. "I don't think so. But you shouldn't quit. You're the best rider I've ever seen."

"I won't quit riding," Ashleigh said. But for the moment she couldn't imagine ever going back to the stable.

"Oh, Chesterton's selling Neptune." Diana balanced carefully on her crutches and brushed her blond hair out of her eyes. "I guess the owner of the stable thought he was too dangerous, after what happened to Caroline."

"But it wasn't his fault. I think any horse would have spooked when that truck backfired," Ashleigh said.

"Well, maybe." Diana frowned. "But Neptune's gone."

"Caro will be sorry he is," Ashleigh said. "I don't think she wanted him to be blamed for what happened."

"Why do you guys care?" Diana asked. "He was just a horse."

Ashleigh was silent. She felt bad about Neptune, and terrible about Silverado.

"Anyway, thanks for everything you did for Silver," Diana said. "Jane told me you were with him almost the whole time."

Ashleigh looked at her. "You're welcome," she said. "I wish we'd been able to help. He was a beautiful horse."

"Yeah, he was," Diana said quietly. For just a moment her expression softened. Then she shrugged again. "Well, see you around."

Ashleigh nodded. She watched Diana limp back to her crowd of friends. "Diana may forget you, Silver, but I won't," she whispered. "I promise. You're too beautiful to forget."

I'm always going to be losing horses, she thought. *I guess I should get used to it.* She glanced back at Diana. Diana was laughing and talking with her friends.

Ashleigh stuffed her uneaten lunch back into the bag and got up. *But it does matter,* she thought.

16

"I GUESS THIS IS GOOD-BYE, SINCE I'M NOT GOING TO BE taking lessons anymore," Ashleigh said to Ranger the next Saturday. She opened the half-door to his stall and walked in. "I just don't want to do this kind of riding. But I'll miss you, boy."

The big chestnut craned his neck around and looked at her curiously. Then he pulled a bite of hay out of his net and chomped contentedly.

"We were starting to like each other so much. And I was just getting used to your tricks." Ashleigh smiled a little. "But you'll have other kids to teach, you know."

Ranger stopped eating and stepped close to her. He sniffed her hands. Ashleigh hugged him tightly around the neck. "Good boy," she said. "I'll never forget what you did for Caroline. Try hard for those other kids like you did for me, okay?" She quickly opened the stall door and walked out. Ranger tried to push out with her.

169

"We're not going for a ride now," Ashleigh said. "But maybe I'll see you again someday." *I'm not very good at saying good-bye,* she thought as she shut the stall door. *I should try to get better at it.*

Ranger put his head over the stall door, watching her.

"Just don't blow up when your next rider tries to saddle you," Ashleigh called, walking backward down the aisle. "No one likes to ride upside down, Ranger."

Ranger snorted and shook his head vigorously. Ashleigh laughed. "I mean it," she said.

As she opened the barn door Ashleigh wondered if she'd ironed any of the tricks out of Ranger. No, she decided. The next rider would have to start all over again. But maybe having a horse full of tricks wasn't a bad part of riding school. Ashleigh knew she'd never have trouble saddling or bridling any horse for the rest of her life.

A fresh, playful breeze blew her hair in her eyes. Ashleigh pushed it back and walked over to one of the outdoor rings. Jane was standing at the center, teaching dressage to a young girl.

"Seat back. Don't neck-rein! This isn't a cow-roping contest!" Jane shouted.

Ashleigh thought the girl would cringe. But she frowned fiercely, then adjusted her seat and hands. Ashleigh smiled. The girl had learned to handle Jane. That was an important lesson, she thought.

Jane saw Ashleigh and waved. Caught by the breeze, the sandy dust in the ring swirled over Ashleigh's boots as she walked across to Jane.

"What's up?" Jane asked, keeping her eyes on the student.

"I wanted to thank you for the lessons," Ashleigh said. "But I won't be coming anymore."

Jane was silent for a moment. "Okay, Alison!" she called. "Walk him out." Jane turned to Ashleigh. "Why?" she asked. "Do you know how much natural ability you have?"

Ashleigh smiled. "Thanks. But I don't think I want to do equitation or jumping."

Jane nodded. "I certainly accept your decision, after what happened here."

Ashleigh hesitated. "I'm not quitting because Silverado died," she said. "I want to work with my horse at home. She's part Thoroughbred, and I like to go fast with her."

"I can understand that, since I'm a steeplechaser." Jane looked at her intently. "Are you going to be a jockey?"

"I want to try." Ashleigh felt her heart beat faster just at the thought of riding in races, the burning speed of the powerful horse beneath her.

"I think you'll make a good jockey," Jane said. "You've got the determination and skill to do anything you want with horses. Well, I enjoyed teaching you. You made this crazy career of mine rewarding for a while."

"Thanks," Ashleigh said. "I learned a lot."

"Come back anytime." Jane gave her a small, crooked smile.

"I will." But Ashleigh knew she would never ride there again.

At the far end of the ring a heavyset, powerful-looking dressage horse was executing a perfect half-pass, moving slowly and gracefully on a diagonal across the ring. The rider wore a coat with long tails and a flat silk hat.

That won't ever be me, Ashleigh thought. *But that's okay.* Ashleigh's steps quickened as she left the ring. She was going home to Stardust.

Mrs. Griffen was waiting in the truck by the gate. She pushed open the door. "Did you have a good lesson?" she asked.

"Sort of," Ashleigh answered evasively. She didn't really want to tell her mother that she'd quit. Ashleigh hated to quit anything.

Mrs. Griffen dropped the subject. After the recent disaster with Silverado at Chesterton, probably nobody expected her to have a great lesson, anyway.

Ashleigh looked out the window as they drove to Edgardale. She could see the barest hint of green in the paddock grass. *It's really getting to be riding weather,* she thought.

They pulled into the driveway at Edgardale. "I'm going to groom Gallantry," Mrs. Griffen said.

"Oh." Ashleigh wondered why her mother would do that in the middle of the day. "Are you going to try riding her again?"

"No, I gave that up." Mrs. Griffen laughed. "She was such a handful the last time I rode, I'm lucky I came back in one piece. I just want to get her cleaned up."

"I'll help you." Ashleigh slowly followed her mother into the barn. She couldn't decide when would be the best time to tell her that she'd quit the riding school.

"I'm going to check our hay supply," Mrs. Griffen said,

climbing the ladder to the hayloft. "We may need to reorder soon. I hope we can make it to the first cutting in spring. The hay will be better then and the prices lower."

Ashleigh looked up at her mother's back. She had a feeling her mother wouldn't be too happy about her decision. After all, the riding school had been her parents' idea in the first place.

Ashleigh took a deep breath. She might as well get it over with. "I've decided to quit at Chesterton," she called up.

Mrs. Griffen looked over the edge of the loft. "Let me finish counting the bales, and then I'll be down. We need to talk about this."

"Okay."

After a few minutes Mrs. Griffen climbed down the ladder. She put her hand on Ashleigh's shoulder. "Are you sure?"

Ashleigh nodded. "Completely."

"But Ashleigh, why do you want to quit?" her mother said with concern. "Jane said you're doing so well. I know you're upset about what happened to the horse over there," she continued softly. "He was a beautiful animal, wasn't he?"

"Yeah." Ashleigh frowned. Her decision to stop taking lessons at Chesterton did have something to do with Silverado's death—Ashleigh had too many bad memories of the place. But that wasn't the real reason. "I just don't want to take lessons right now," she said. "I think I'd rather ride Stardust around the farm with Mona and work with our horses."

Mrs. Griffen nodded. "It's much easier—and probably

afer—to ride and work with your own horses. Let me get Gallantry."

Mrs. Griffen walked to Gallantry's stall and led the mare to the crossties. As usual, Gallantry snorted and shied, pulling at the lead rope and dancing her hindquarters in a semicircle.

Ashleigh wondered if she should tell her mother that she was quitting the lessons not to be safer but because she wanted to be a jockey. Stardust was over half Thoroughbred and a lot closer to a racehorse than Ranger.

No, she decided. *Mom will try to talk me out of it because it's so dangerous, especially after what happened to Caroline. I'll tell her sometime soon, after I've shown everybody what I can do with Stardust.*

"At your age it's hard to know what you really want," Mrs. Griffen said, picking up a dandy brush. "Think a little more about the riding school before you give it up, Ashleigh."

"Okay," Ashleigh said. *But I won't change my mind,* she thought. *Not a chance.*

"Maybe I can start teaching you," Mrs. Griffen said. "Things are going so well at Edgardale, I may be able to quit my office job soon."

Ashleigh nodded. "That's great." She was sure she could learn a lot about riding from her mom. But she also knew she could learn a lot from Stardust—about the sheer joy of flying like the wind, and how to control speed. "I'm going out for a ride with Mona," she said.

"Sounds like fun," Mrs. Griffen said. "Oh, Ashleigh—I wanted to tell you. . . ."

"What?" Ashleigh looked at her mother. Mrs. Griffen had a funny expression on her face—half sad, half expectant. She looked back at Gallantry. The bay mare was lightly pawing the aisle.

"We're selling Gallantry," Mrs. Griffen said. "I'm getting her ready to leave today. She's going back to racing."

"Oh," Ashleigh said slowly. "That's good." She felt a rush of conflicting emotions. She didn't want the spirited mare to leave the farm. *But Gallantry will be happier at the track,* Ashleigh thought. *She hasn't wanted to do anything but run since she got here.* "I'll miss her," she said.

"I know you will." Mrs. Griffen smiled sadly. "But we got a very good offer for her. I think we did the right thing. Won't it be something to see her race again?"

"It'll be great." Ashleigh remembered Gallantry's blazing finish at Churchill Downs back in October. Gallantry had grown up since then—now she was probably even faster. Ashleigh half closed her eyes for a moment, picturing the bay mare roaring down the track the way she had in the paddock, on the way to a spectacular finish.

Ashleigh opened her eyes. "I think I'll go see Stardust now," she said.

Mrs. Griffen nodded. "Good idea. It's a beautiful day for a ride."

Ashleigh walked out to the paddock, tilting her head to let the warm, soothing rays of the sun touch her face. *I might see a new foal,* she thought. Several of the mares were due any day.

Stardust was grazing with Moe in the side paddock.

She jerked up her head when she saw Ashleigh and with a whinny of greeting trotted over to the fence.

Ashleigh felt a rush of pride. The brilliant sun turned Stardust's gleaming coat to solid copper. The graceful mare seemed to float through the air, her strides long and easy on her slender legs. Behind her Moe cantered to keep up.

Stardust skidded to a stop and poked her head over the gate. She seemed to be saying, *Hurry up!*

Ashleigh broke into a run. "I'm coming, girl!"

Moe waited at the gate with Stardust. It almost broke Ashleigh's heart the way the small pony stood there expectantly, so confident that she had come to get him for a ride. He didn't understand that he'd been replaced.

"I can't take you today, boy," Ashleigh said. She pushed the pony's thick forelock aside and pressed her cheek to his forehead. "We're going to go too fast. Rory will come ride you soon."

Moe nudged the gate.

"I know you don't understand," Ashleigh said. "But you'll have fun again soon, I promise." Deftly Ashleigh maneuvered Stardust out of the gate while keeping Moe inside.

"I've been thinking a lot lately, Stardust," she told the mare as they walked up to the barn. "Someday I'm going to be a jockey."

Stardust pricked her ears.

"Maybe I'm crazy to want to," Ashleigh went on. "It's so hard and dangerous. Even more than ordinary riding." Ashleigh closed her eyes briefly, picturing both the terrible scene with Caroline and Silverado's pain. She shook her head. "I won't think about that anymore. I've got work to do."

Ashleigh crosstied Stardust in the barn and walked into the tack room. She picked up the mare's bridle and saddle. Mona was probably on her way over with Frisky. The girls planned to race along the lane. That day they would see just how much speed their horses had.

Stardust pawed the concrete aisle and strained against the crossties.

"You know what's coming, don't you?" Ashleigh smiled. "This will be good. Let's just give you a brushing, then we'll go."

A cool breeze fanned Ashleigh's face as she led Stardust into the stable yard. It smelled of melting snow. Ashleigh noticed that the daffodils were sprouting next to the barn wall. Soon they would bear brilliant yellow star-shaped flowers.

"Ash!" Rory yelled from the path to the paddock. "I'm going to ride Moe—come watch!"

"Ask Mom to watch you!" Ashleigh called. "I'll help you when I get back." *Good,* she thought. *Now that I know Moe will be okay, my ride will be just perfect.*

The clear, happy calls of the first spring robins rang out from nearby trees as she and Stardust trotted down the drive and turned onto the lane. Stardust jumped lightly over a small branch. "You know it's almost spring, don't you?" Ashleigh said with a chuckle.

A van that read SANTERVILLE FARMS on the side was rolling slowly up the drive. *Gallantry's new owners,* Ashleigh thought.

"Good-bye, girl," she called softly. "See you at the track. You're going to run so fast!"

Mrs. Griffen led Gallantry out of the barn. Ashleigh felt a rush of pure joy at the thought of the mare's racing again. *Not all good-byes are bad,* she said to herself.

At the edge of the woods Mona was waiting on Frisky. "Is today race day?" she asked with a grin.

"You bet. We've never run these two against each other. Let's canter to the top of the lane to warm up, then gallop them back toward Edgardale." Ashleigh clucked to Stardust, urging her into a canter.

Stardust cantered for a few strides. Then, as if she knew they were about to race, she shifted gears into a smooth gallop. At the top of the lane Ashleigh stopped Stardust and turned her.

The mare pulled hard against the reins, eager to be off.

"Just a second," Ashleigh said, laughing. Mona stopped Frisky beside them.

"Where should we start the race? Right here?" Mona asked.

"No, let's ease them into it. Let's gallop to that tree down there"—Ashleigh shaded her eyes against the sun and pointed—"then let them all the way out." Below them were the rolling, grassy paddocks of Edgardale, framed by bare trees. In the stable yard Ashleigh could see Rory circling Moe.

Stardust pranced in place, tossing her head. "Just a second, girl," Ashleigh said, checking the mare with the reins. She looked ahead to the tree, calculating how much she should let Stardust out before they got there.

"Nervous?" Mona asked.

Ashleigh shook her head. "This is going to be too much fun for me to be nervous."

The girls lined up their horses and looked at each other. "Okay?" Ashleigh said.

Mona nodded and gripped her reins tightly.

"Ready, set—go, Stardust!" Ashleigh called, and clucked to the mare. Stardust took off with a tremendous lunge, switching instantly into a gallop.

The wind roared in Ashleigh's ears as Stardust's hooves beat a quickening tattoo on the hard ground. Ashleigh felt nothing but sheer exhilaration from the speed of the ride. Stardust was going faster and faster on her own, as if she knew exactly what Ashleigh wanted.

The tree at the start of the race flashed by. Ashleigh glanced over her shoulder. Frisky was giving the race all she was worth. The light bay mare was pounding at Stardust's flank.

But not for long, Ashleigh thought. Stardust's ears flicked back. She was waiting for Ashleigh's signal.

"You love racing, don't you, girl?" Ashleigh called. "So do I. I want to feel like this for the rest of my life!"

Ashleigh crouched over Stardust's neck, burying her hands in the horse's thick, silky mane. "Run, Stardust!" she cried. "Win it!" The chestnut mare changed leads and leaped ahead, powering for the finish.

JOANNA CAMPBELL was born and raised in Norwalk, Connecticut and grew up loving horses. She eventually owned a horse of her own and took riding lessons for a number of years, specializing in jumping. She still rides when possible and has started her three-year-old granddaughter on lessons. In addition to publishing over twenty-five novels for young adults, she is the author of four adult novels. She has also sung and played piano professionally and owned an antique business. She now lives on the coast of Maine in Camden with her husband, Ian Bruce. She has two children, Kimberly and Kenneth, and three grandchildren.

KAREN BENTLEY rode in English equitation and jumping classes as a child and in Western equitation and barrel-racing classes as a teenager. She has bred and raised Quarter Horses and, during a sojourn on the East Coast, owned a half-Thoroughbred jumper. She now owns a red roan registered Quarter Horse with some reining moves and lives in New Mexico. She has published five novels for young adults.